S0-ADS-645

frost

<u>Other books by Kate Avery Ellison</u>

The Curse Girl

Once Upon a Beanstalk

frost

Kate Avery Ellison

Copyright © 2012 Kate Avery Ellison

All Rights Reserved

Do not distribute or copy this book, in print or electronic format, in part or in whole, without the written consent of the author.

ISBN: 1475005873

ISBN-13: 978-1475005875

For Scott

Without you, none of this would be possible.

I love you.

ONE

IT WAS COLD, the kind of cold that made bones feel brittle and hands ache. My breath streamed from my lips like smoke, and my feet made wet, crunching sounds in the snow as I slipped through the forest. As I ran, my lungs ached and my sack of yarn thumped against my back. My cloak tangled around my ankles, but I yanked it free without stopping.

It was quota day in the village, and I was going to be late if I didn't hurry.

The path stretched ahead in a white trail of unbroken snow, and on either side the ice-covered limbs of the trees hemmed me in with walls of frosty green. Even the light took on a grim, almost gray-blue quality here, and the world was blank with silence. I could hear only the ragged noise of my own breathing and my own footsteps. I felt like an interloper—too loud, too clumsy, too disruptive.

The Frost was always like that. The snow-covered trees had a deadening effect. They absorbed everything—animal calls, voices, even screams for help. Something could come from behind without warning, and you wouldn't hear anything until it was right upon you. Until it was almost too late.

A branch snapped in the woods to my left. I flinched, turning my head in an effort to locate the source of the sound.

But silence wrapped the world once more. The shadows lay still and gray across the snow. Empty.

"It's still light," I whispered aloud, trying to reassure myself. In the light, I was safe. Even the smallest child knew that much.

The monsters didn't come out until after dark.

I moved faster anyway, spooked by that branch snap even though a blue-gray gloom still illuminated the path. A shiver ran down my spine. Despite our often-repeated mantras about the safety of the light, nothing was certain in the Frost. My parents had always been careful. They had always been prepared. And yet, two months ago they went out into the Frost in the daylight and never returned.

They'd been found days later, dead.

They'd been killed by the monsters that lurked deep in the Frost, monsters that barely anyone ever saw except for tracks in the snow, or the glow of their red eyes in the darkness.

My people called them Watchers.

Color danced at the edges of my vision as I passed the winter-defying snow blossoms, their long sky-blue petals drooping with ice as they dangled from the bushes that lined the path. They were everywhere here, spilling across the snow, drawing a line of demarcation between me and the woods. Every winter, the snows came and the cold killed everything, but these flowers lived. We planted them everywhere—on the paths and around our houses—because the Watchers rarely crossed a fallen snow blossom. For some reason, the flowers turned them away.

Usually.

8

I touched the bunch that dangled from my throat with one finger. My parents' snow blossom necklaces had been missing from their bodies when they were found. Had the monsters torn the flowers off before killing them, or had they even been wearing them at all?

Another branch snapped behind me, the crack loud as a shout in the stillness.

I hurried faster.

Sometimes we found tracks across the paths despite the blossoms. Sometimes nothing kept the Watchers out.

My foot caught a root, and I stumbled.

The bushes rustled behind me.

Panic clawed at my throat. I dropped my sack, fumbling at my belt for the knife I carried even though I knew it would do no good against the monsters because no weapons stopped them. I turned, ready to defend myself.

The branches parted, and a figure stepped onto the path.

It was only Cole, one of the village boys.

"Cole," I snapped, sheathing the knife. "Are you trying to kill me with fright?"

He flashed me a sheepish smile. "Did you think I was a Watcher, Lia?"

I threw a glance at the sky as I snatched up my sack and flung it over my shoulder once more. Clouds were rolling in, blocking out the sun. The light around us was growing dimmer, filling the path with a premature twilight. A storm was coming.

His smile faded a little at my expression. "I'm sorry," he said. "I should have called out to warn you."

"We're supposed to stay on the paths," I growled, brushing snow from my skirt. I didn't want to discuss my irrational panic. I'd been walking the paths through

9

the Frost my entire life. I shouldn't be jumping at every stray sound like some five-year-old child.

Cole pointed at two squirrel pelts dangling from his belt. "Quota," he said simply, adjusting the bow hanging on his back. He moved past me and onto the path. "Speaking of which, we're going to be late for the counting."

"You're a Carver," I said, falling into step beside him. "Not a Hunter."

"And you're a Weaver, not a Farmer, but you still keep horses and chickens," he said.

I shrugged, still annoyed with him for startling me. "My parents took that farm because no one else wanted it. It's too far from the village, too isolated. We keep animals because we have room. I don't bring them into the village on quota day."

"The quota master gives my family a little extra flour if I slip him a pelt," Cole said. He glanced down at me, his smile mysterious. "Besides, the forest isn't dangerous this close to the village, not in daylight."

"The Frost is always dangerous," I said firmly.

Cole tipped his head to one side and smiled. He refrained from disagreeing outright out of politeness, I supposed. Having dead parents usually evoked that response from people. "I can take care of myself," he said.

I looked him over. He was tall, and he carried the bow like he knew how to use it. He might be called handsome by some, but he was too lean and foxlike for my taste. He had a daring streak a mile wide, and his eyes always seemed to hold some secret. His mouth slid into a smirk between every word he spoke.

Our gazes held a moment, and his eyes narrowed with sudden decision. For some reason, his expression unnerved me.

"Lia—"

"We're going to be late," I said, dodging, and hurried ahead.

I could hear him jogging to catch up as I rounded the curve. Here the path crawled beneath a leaning pair of massive boulders and alongside a stream of dark, turbulent water. I scrambled around the first rock, but then what I saw on the other side of the river made me freeze.

Shadowy figures in gray uniforms slipped through the trees, rifles in their hands. There were two of them, sharp-eyed and dark-haired. Bandoleers glittered across their chests.

Cole caught up with me. I put up a hand to quiet him, and together we watched.

"Farthers," I whispered.

"What are they doing this close to the Frost?" Cole muttered.

I just shook my head as a shiver descended my spine. Farthers—the people from farther than the Frost—rarely ventured beyond the place where the snow and ice began. They had their own country, a grim and gray place called Aeralis, and we knew only rumors of it, but those rumors were enough to inspire fear in us all. I'd been as far as the roads that ringed their land once. I'd seen the horse-drawn wagons filled with prisoners, and the sharp metal fences that marred the fields like stitches across a pale white cheek.

The men crept down to the bank and stared at the dark water. They hadn't seen us. One gestured at the river, and another pointed at the sky and the approaching storm clouds that were visible through the break in the trees. They appeared to be arguing.

"They won't cross the river," I said, confident of it despite my fear. "They never do."

11

"They're afraid of Watchers," Cole said.

I laughed under my breath at the irony of it. The monsters in the woods protected us as much as they endangered us.

After another moment, the Farthers went back up the bank and vanished into the trees. Like I'd predicted, they didn't cross the river into our lands. I sighed.

Cole spat at the ground in disgust. "Those Farther scum."

I didn't reply. Another glance at the sky confirmed that the storm was fast approaching with the night, and our time was dwindling. We still had to deliver our quota.

I turned back to the path and ran for the village.

TWO

THE WOODEN ROOFS of the village began to poke above the evergreen trees, and some of my anxiety eased.

Almost there.

I struggled down the steep hill that led to the gate, my feet slipping on icy rocks. The sack in my hand bumped against my thigh. Cole was right behind me, his boots crunching against the snow.

When I reached the bottom, I brushed twigs off my cloak and hurried through the wooden gate with its faded etchings and carved name of the village—Iceliss. Nobody called it that, though. It was simply our village, *the* village. There was nothing else here in the Frost but us.

Inside the village proper, people clothed in the muted colors of a snowy forest swarmed everywhere. Their arms overflowed with the goods they were bringing to satisfy their quota, the weekly work their family was assigned by the village Elders. Children ran past me with bundles of firewood, baker women balanced baskets of steaming loaves, and fishermen carried strings of fish that they'd pulled from beneath the icy lakes and streams. I left Cole behind as I shoved through the throng, heading for the center of town and the quota master who would mark my name off the list and give me my earned weekly supplies of salt, sugar, and grain.

I reached the line just outside the Assembly Hall and glanced again at the sky. The clouds were still piling up like dirty wool on the horizon. The storm was fast approaching, and getting home might be difficult.

My stomach squeezed with fresh worry. I shouldn't have come so late. But my sister hadn't done her chores, and I'd lost track of time while finishing them for her.

"Lia Weaver," the quota master called. He looked from the list to my face.

I stepped forward, presenting him my sack, and he pulled out the contents and glanced them over. My face grew hot as he scrutinized the mess of yarn—I hadn't even had time to roll it into the neat balls I normally did—but he didn't comment. He handed me the sack of supplies that I had earned, and relief slipped down my spine as I accepted it. I turned to leave, enjoying the heavy feel of the sack in my hand.

"Lia!"

My friend Ann Mayor leaned over the stone fence that edged the Assembly Yard, her face framed by a bright red hood. Village dwellers didn't always wear the muted blues, whites, and browns of the forest like those who roamed the paths of the Frost. The villagers didn't have to, because they stayed safe behind the high walls.

"Ann." A twinge of something like apprehension touched me at the sight of her, because she'd been avoiding me lately and I didn't know why. The muddy snow that covered the ground crunched beneath my boots as I hurried across the yard to her side.

"Are you well?" Her eyes searched my face. "You look frightened."

"I saw a few Farthers across the river," I said. I didn't mention my silly panic on the paths, or Cole's annoying advances that made me squirm with discomfort.

14

She closed her eyes briefly at the mention of Farthers. "Oh." Farthers were not something anybody liked to discuss, but Ann had a special terror of them.

"They went away," I added quickly. "They always do."

She bent forward and lowered her voice a little as she changed the subject. "I didn't see you at Assembly last week."

I flushed. The weekly Assembly was necessary so each household would know the quota and supply levels, which fluctuated with the needs of the village. We were all cogs in the machine, doing our parts with our individual quota output to keep the village production at its peak. Order, production, discipline, rules...without them, we would starve in the harsh winters and bleak summers.

One adult member of each household was required to attend each week, and since my parents were dead, the responsibility fell to me. But our farm was at the very brink of our small civilization, and the trek into town was cold and dangerous. Sometimes I didn't go.

"I'm sorry. My sister was being difficult like always. She wanders off and forgets her chores. I barely made quota this week—"

Normally I wouldn't throw my silly sister to the wolves, even if my lateness was her fault, but Ann was my friend. She knew how Ivy could be. We often shared an exasperated laugh at our younger siblings' expense.

But this time, Ann only frowned at my excuse. She bit her lip and looked over her shoulder. "The Elders noticed, Lia. My father noticed."

A shiver of suspicion tickled the back of my neck. As the daughter of our village leader, she had access to information that I did not, like whether or not the Elders really thought I was capable of taking care of my siblings now that my parents were gone.

"Did they say something?"

A faint blush spread across her cheeks. "I can't...I really shouldn't be talking about this. I just wanted to tell you to be sure to do your part, that's all. Important people are watching."

My stomach twisted into a knot. If the Elders thought I was unfit to take care of my siblings, we'd be separated for sure. "I'll be there this week, Ann, I promise. Thank you for telling me."

She nodded, and the curls framing her delicate face quivered.

I glanced at the sky again. The clouds were closer, and the light was growing grayer. Time to head back to the farm. "I must be going—"

"Lia Weaver," another voice interrupted loudly from across the yard, and I turned to see Everiss Dyer, a curvaceous brunette with a loud voice and perpetually stained hands from her family's profession, sashaying toward us. She'd always been more Ann's friend than mine, but I gritted my teeth into a smile and nodded to her.

"Hello, Everiss."

Everiss brushed purple-stained fingers over her hood, which was not nearly as fine as Ann's embroidered one. But it was ten times nicer than my ragged, ice-blue cloak with the fraying seams. I could see her mentally making the comparison, and I dropped my eyes.

"Did you hear the news?" she asked me.

I shook my head.

Ann and Everiss exchanged wistful glances. "The Tailor family's oldest son announced his intentions,"

16

Everiss said, wetting her lips with her tongue. "Can you imagine it? Me, courting? And such an older man..."

"Don't be silly," Ann said with a laugh. "He's less than a year older than you, you goose."

They both looked at me for my reaction. I forced a smile and nodded, trying to feign enthusiasm. Good for her. Making a match and forming a family was one of the most important things anyone could do here in the Frost. It ensured your survival. It ensured your place in the village. It was every girl's dream, I supposed.

It was my secret dread.

"Don't look so jealous," Everiss said, smirking as she misinterpreted my expression. "Your time will come."

She and Ann both shifted their gaze to someplace over my shoulder. "Speaking of which..." Ann said, giving me a conspiratorial smile.

I turned. Cole Carver was heading straight for us, his sack of supplies in one hand and his cloak flapping behind him. Here in the village, he looked more ridiculous than mysterious.

"Ann..." I said, sighing.

"He likes you," she murmured. "He's always asking about you."

Cole reached us and stopped, smirking at me just like he'd done in the forest. "Hello, girls. Hello again, Lia."

"Again?" Everiss arched her eyebrows.

"Lia and I ran into one another on one of the forest paths. We walked here together."

I was suddenly uncomfortable with the way Everiss and Ann were grinning at me. I gestured at the sky. "A storm is coming. I really should get back to the farm—" I edged away, trying to escape their predatory matchmaking attempts.

17

Ever since I'd been orphaned, every idle villager had decided I was in need of a husband, it seemed. I was sick of it.

Everiss blocked my way. "If you'd been at the last Assembly, you would have heard that there's going to be a winter social next month."

Ann's gaze shifted from me to Cole. "Do you think you'll attend?"

"I don't know," I said irritably. "My brother and sister..."

I didn't have to finish the thought. Everyone understood. Freshly orphaned, with a cripple brother and an impetuous younger sister, I had my hands full without counting quota and the upkeep of the farm. If anyone had a reason to skip socializing, it was me.

The wind blew between us, and a few snowflakes brushed my face.

"I should get back to the farm," I said again. I began to walk, and this time they followed instead of trying to stop me.

The girls murmured together about the social while Cole fell into step beside me. The village streets had already begun to empty as the weather drove people indoors. Unencumbered, we passed the houses of stone and wood with their narrow, rounded doors and shuttered windows. I saw a merchant from the south in the streets. Trinkets and gadgets made of cogs and gears from Aeralis and the Dark Lands to the south covered his chest and hung from his belt. A shiver rippled over my skin. Carrying things with that kind of technology in the Frost was dangerous. Didn't he know?

"I wish you would come," Cole persisted. He was matching my strides with his, and with each step the shock of brown hair on his forehead bounced. "We hardly ever get any fun around here. It's good for a body to have some relaxation."

I sighed. I was tired of making excuses. "The farm absorbs most of my time and energy now."

Cole followed my eyes to the merchant, who was now heading toward the gates of the village. I frowned as I realized the man intended to head deeper into the Frost tonight.

"Surely he knows better than to go out there with those Farther things strapped to his chest?" I muttered.

Cole frowned. "Fool. He'll be eaten by the Watchers for sure."

I winced, thinking of my parents. Cole was oblivious to the distress his words had caused me as he watched the disaster unfolding before us.

But before the merchant could slip out the gates, a slender, dark-haired figure stepped forward and pressed a hand against his chest, intercepting him. My lungs squeezed tight, because I recognized the second figure at once.

Cole drew in a sharp breath. "What is that scum doing here?"

"He has quota just like everyone else," I said quietly. I watched as the young man pointed toward the inn and then at the Farther things the merchant carried. He mimed burying them, and his lips moved as he explained the danger. He was too far away to hear, but I knew what he was saying—the creatures in the forest were drawn to the strange technology from the south, one of the reasons we had so little of it. Anyone carrying it in the forest at night would be hunted for sure. He was explaining to the merchant what would happen if he left the village now, with darkness approaching.

19

A sigh slid from my lips. Was this some kind of act to make us think he cared what happened to people out there?

I knew from personal experience that the opposite was true.

"I can't believe him," Cole continued viciously. "Your parents' graves are barely cold, and still he walks around as if we've all forgotten the part his family played in their deaths."

Ann and Everiss broke off their conversation and drew closer. "What is it?" Ann asked, seeing our expressions.

"That idiot Adam Brewer is here," Cole said. "Acting as if nothing is wrong."

Ann avoided looking at me as she spoke. "We don't know that his family is responsible for what happened to Lia's parents. We don't know what happened that day—"

"We know enough," Cole interrupted. He scowled.

"Please," I said. "I don't really want to discuss it."

"Hello, Lia."

I looked up quickly.

Adam Brewer.

He'd left the merchant heading for the inn and approached us instead—had he heard our words about him? My face flushed. My friends were frozen in quiet. Beside me, Cole's eyes narrowed, and I saw his jaw twitch out of the corner of my eye.

But Adam was looking only at me. I straightened my shoulders. I would not cower under his gaze, even though it was wild and sharp as a hawk's.

He was slender, with dark hair that fell into his eyes, and he wore a thick blue cloak as ragged as mine. We were both from farms outside the village walls. Like

20

me, he knew the dangers of the forest because he experienced them firsthand.

Adam's eyes cut to others and then back to mine. "I hope your farm has been free of Watchers lately?"

The word slid through the air, sharp as a knife blade. I sucked in a sharp breath. He was waiting for me to speak to him about the vicious creatures that prowled our forests at night as casually as we might speak of the weather.

I could just say it. *No, I haven't seen any Watchers. And I won't be so foolish as to trust you to protect me from them, either.* The words burned hot on my tongue, but I couldn't spit them out.

My friends shuffled their feet, looking at him with thinly disguised hostility. Nothing had been proven, and there were no charges made against the family, but it was clear what everyone thought. And now here he was, bringing up that word—*Watchers*—like nothing was wrong.

The Brewers were part of the village just like everyone else, but they were not originally from the Frost, and their skin just tanned enough to keep everyone from forgetting that fact. They kept to themselves and didn't mingle much. Although nobody had really liked them before, after my parents' deaths they were regarded with open contempt. They'd asked my parents to help them with their quota and then abandoned them in the forest when the Watchers attacked. And my parents had not come back alive.

He was still looking at me like he expected a response. I hesitated, the words sticking in my throat. A hot, humming pressure started at the back of my head and crept forward—the promise of a headache. I couldn't do it.

21

Lowering my head, I moved past him without speaking. The others followed.

Cole threw a glance over his shoulder. "Idiot."

Shock still reverberated through my body at the near-confrontation. I turned my head to see if the Brewer boy was still standing there, but he'd vanished deeper into the village.

"That was bizarre," Ann said, rushing to agree, to comfort me as we reached the village perimeter and the wall that surrounded it. "My father says the Brewers are a strange bunch."

"They're practically Farthers," Cole spat.

Everyone flinched, and I thought of the soldiers we'd seen earlier. We knew little about the steely eyed people and their land to the south of us, but what we did know was enough. The stories that passed into our village told of arrested citizens, of public brutality, of wealthy who tormented the poor and prisoners who were forced to work as slaves. It was a cruel, cold land of advanced technology and regressed morality. Mothers told their children to be good or the Farthers would steal them away. As a little girl, I'd had nightmares about them.

"Those are strong words, Cole Carver," Ann said sharply. She was loyal to me, but she was also the Mayor's daughter, and a diplomat. "The Brewers are a part of this town, members of our community. They deserve to be treated as such."

He crossed his arms. "They're not from here, same as Farthers."

"Farthers," she said, "Are vicious, cruel people. Comparing anyone in the village to them is a reprehensible accusation—"

"What the Brewers did to Lia's parents was reprehensible, too."

22

I didn't really want to talk about the Brewers or the death of my parents, especially not with Cole. "I have to go," I said, interrupting them. "The storm is getting close."

Cole pressed his lips together and nodded. I think he could finally tell he'd offended me. "May you have clear skies home," he muttered. It was our village's traditional—and cautionary—farewell.

Ann hugged me, and Everiss waved. Together they turned for their homes.

I stepped to the gate and lifted the sack to my shoulder. The wind swept around me, tugging at my hood and the hair beneath. I took a breath and started down the path again.

The forest had already begun to grow dark. Shadows darkened the trail ahead, tricking my eyes and transforming the trees into monstrous shapes with skeletal arms that clawed at the sky. Flurries of snow were beginning to drift down like feathers.

I'd tarried too long, and now I'd have to make the journey home in the grim twilight.

Gathering my cloak and my courage around me, I stepped through the gates.

~

If the journey into the village in daylight was bad, the trip back in near-night was a terror-filled nightmare. The trees seemed to crowd the path like skeletal spectators. Shadows blanketed everything in deep shades of gray. The wind moaned across the snowdrifts, making them hiss.

Something sprang from the darkness to my left. A rabbit. I clapped a hand over my thudding heart and pressed on, fumbling for the flowers at my throat. My

23

skin prickled with every step I took, because with every step the shadows grew deeper and colder. Snowflakes began to swirl, making patterns in the wind and brushing against my cheeks like wet feathers.

The path wound on, and I followed it grimly. Lanterns filled with the glowing fungus found deep in the Frost cast circles of blue light across the snow here and there, their light like fading stars. Some helpful soul had placed them on the path earlier today. The phosphorus-rich fungi would glow for days after picked, but the falling snow made it difficult to see.

Shadows rippled ahead, and the snow crunched. I paused on the path, reaching again for the flowers at my throat. Watchers?

The sound ebbed. I exhaled sharply and pressed on. The incident with Adam Brewer in the village had made me jumpy.

Our farm was the last stop on the path. Ours was the final fingernail on the hand of civilization—after our shabby barn and ramshackle house, there was nothing but icy rocks and trees between us and Aeralis.

Rocks, trees, and Watchers.

I didn't realize I'd been holding my breath until I crested the hill and caught a glimpse of the yellow light streaming through the windows of the farmhouse. My head cleared and I sighed as if I'd just broken the surface of a deep lake. An unexpected flare of emotion squeezed my chest and prickled at the corners of my eyes. Blinking hard against it, I checked the sky again and then went to the barn to see to the animals. I rarely cried, because what good did crying do? Yet seeing Adam Brewer in the village had dredged up a whirl of emotions in me.

There was no time to stew on it, though. I brought the horses in from their paddock and fed and watered them. I checked the hens to be sure they were warm and settled in their coop at the back of the barn. I rubbed my fingers over the bridge of the cow's nose and down her side before dumping the bucket of dried turnips into her feed trough. They didn't have names, any of them, because I saw no sense in naming the food. The cow and the chickens would be slaughtered for meat when they were too old, and the horses were not really ours. They belonged to the village, but we stabled them. They were a matched pair, small and shaggy and fleet-footed.

Satisfied that the animals were settled for the night, I returned to the yard. Little shards of ice stabbed my skin and prickled against my cheeks. On the porch, the Watcher Ward over the door clattered and turned in the wind, the blue ribbons and carved wooden snow blossom symbols making a tinkle of ominous music above my head. I opened the door to the house and went in.

The house was too hot after the freezing wind, and the air smelled like warm milk and baked apples. The fire on the hearth blazed high. I tossed my cloak across the hook by the entrance and put the bag of supplies in the kitchen. "Jonn? Ivy?"

My brother Jonn raised his head from the yarn in his lap at my entrance. He looked just like me—lanky limbs, a narrow, shrewd face framed by pale, red-blond hair, a stubborn sweep of freckles across his nose and cheeks like speckles on a bird's egg. We were twins, and we looked it.

"Where's Ivy?" I swept my gaze across the main room of the house. Dried laundry draped across my great-grandmother's furniture, laundry my little sister had been supposed to fold and put away before I got home. A curl of anger kindled in the pit of my stomach— we were barely making quota, the winter storms were

25

upon us, and she wasn't even keeping up with the basic chores I gave her. She was almost fourteen—she was old enough to do her share of the work.

Jonn raised his eyebrows. "I haven't seen her all afternoon. I thought she was with you."

A little piece of my insides froze at his words. Our eyes met and held, and a million wordless things passed between us. I went back to the door and opened it.

Darkness was falling along with the snow. I hadn't seen my sister in the village, and she hadn't been in the barn. It was a small farm—just a round clearing in the woods, really. There was no sign of her in the yard. I shouted her name, but the wind snatched the word from my lips and flung it away. The Watcher Ward rattled above me, and the sound was like bones shaking.

My heart beat fast. My lungs were suddenly empty. I took a shaky breath and then exhaled slowly before turning to my brother.

"I'm going out to find her."

Jonn looked at the fire. I knew he wouldn't argue with me—he wasn't the type to voice disagreements, especially not with me—but his whole face tightened and his lips turned white. "The Watchers..."

"It's too early for Watchers to be out," I said. "There's still light left. Besides, nobody's seen one in months."

That was a half-lie, as their tracks were spotted almost every week crisscrossing the paths or wandering around the edges of the village where the border of snow blossoms was planted to keep them out. But it was a half-truth, too. We hadn't seen them recently.

But Jonn and I knew better than anybody that there was still a risk.

"I'm going," I said.

26

He didn't reply, but I could tell by his expression that he was furious that he couldn't go. He wasn't mad at me. It was just the way things were. There was no point in wasting time talking about it, so we didn't.

I pulled on my cloak again and struggled into my heavy boots with the snowshoes for walking on top of the snow. Opening the front door, I threw one final look over my shoulder at Jonn before ducking back out into the wintery evening.

It had grown colder since I'd been inside, or maybe that was just the wind stealing the warmth from my body. I padded through the dusting of snow that covered everything, cupping my hands over my mouth to call her again. "Ivy!"

Most of the time fear was just like a rat in my belly, gnawing and gnawing a hole in the same place day after day whenever I'd let it. But now the rat had turned into a lion, and it was tearing me apart from the inside out. I reached the edge of the yard, where the trees formed a wall of brown and green, and I stopped. The wind shivered through my hair.

"Ivy!" I screamed again.

She was always wandering the farm with a dream in her eyes and a song in her mouth. She had a head full of thoughts about things that didn't matter and never would, and she didn't have an ounce of sense when it came to our survival. I wrapped both arms tight around my middle to hold in the fear, and I sucked in another breath to call again when I heard it, lost against the wind. My name.

"Lia...?"

Her voice was faint, almost imperceptible, but my ears were fine-tuned with terror and I heard it. I surged forward into the woods, kicking up snow. "Ivy?"

27

She appeared out of the shadows suddenly. Her cheeks were bitten red with cold and her long dark hair was wet with melting ice. She stumbled, grabbed my hands. Her mittens were missing. "Hurry," she breathed, tugging at me. "Quickly."

"Ivy Augusta Weaver," I hissed, torn between joyful relief and flickering anger. "It's almost night time. There is a storm coming. What were you thinking? Where have you been?"

"There is a boy," she panted, ignoring my scolding. "In the woods."

"What?"

But she was already plunging deeper into the forest, and I had no choice but to follow her, a new worry filling my mind and replacing the short-lived relief I'd felt. A boy in the woods? Who had gotten himself lost in the woods at a time like this? One of the farmers' sons, perhaps?

We were the last farm in the Frost. There was nothing beyond us to the north but the Empty, and to the south there was only the Farther World. What was anybody doing at the edge of that?

Ivy and I continued into the forest. We ducked around branches and scrambled over icy roots. The shadows were thick, and they painted our cloaks a deep indigo.

Ivy reached a giant rock at the mouth of a clearing and stopped. "There," she said, pointing with a trembling hand.

I could just make out the crumpled form. In my anxiety, I saw only isolated details. A thin, wet shirt, a pair of shoulders, a face almost hidden by the snow. I took a step forward, trying to place the face...and then I saw the sharp features, the dark hair, the slightly tanned tone of the skin. I halted as my blood turned stone-cold.

28

Time became protracted and dense, like swimming underwater. Sound was muffled. My chest felt tight.

You must be strong, Lia. My mother's voice rang in my head. I remembered her wind-weathered face, her chapped hands gripping mine, her earnest eyes as they scoured my face for weakness. There could be no weakness here in the Frost, where we clung to life between the mountains as desperately as a drowning man clings to a stone.

"He's not one of ours," I said, turning to her with sudden fierceness. "Ivy..."

"He's hurt," she said.

"Don't you understand?"

She just looked at me. I drew in a deep breath.

"*That* is a Farther."

THREE

IVY'S EYES WIDENED a fraction at my harsh words. The wind blew between us, spraying ice against our faces. She blinked. I didn't.

"A...a Farther?"

Of course she knew what that was—every person in our village knew who the Farthers were, even those who'd never caught a glimpse of them across the river. We barely ever spoke of them, but they inhabited everyone's nightmares all the same.

I nodded curtly.

Ivy struggled to understand what I was implying. "But he's hurt," she managed, as if that was the only concern. "And it's getting dark."

"We must protect ourselves," I said.

Ivy swallowed hard.

I glared at her. "No."

She looked back at the figure lying in the snow. I glanced at the sky again, trying to calculate how much time we had left before the sun sunk completely behind the trees, and we were no longer safe from the things that prowled in the darkness. The Watchers never moved across our yards or around the town perimeter during the sunlight hours, but some had reported seeing them during the narrow span of twilight that joined the day and the night, and it was rumored that they wandered freely in the deep of the forests even during the day.

The wind howled through the trees and tugged at my cloak. Snow fell sideways.

"But he's hurt," Ivy whispered again, breaking into my thoughts.

I closed my eyes briefly. My sister was the kind of person who brought home baby birds who'd fallen from their nests and raccoons with thorns in their paws. But we couldn't simply take a Farther and bandage him up like a lost puppy. "The Elders say—"

"I know they're dangerous. I know what the Elders say." Ivy's voice was as brittle as ice. "But are you telling me you're going to leave him out here to die? After what happened to Ma and Da?"

I bit my lip so hard I tasted blood. Ivy looked at me with her big brown eyes and the fear in my gut snarled. What would the villagers say? *This is dangerous,* my mind screamed at me. *This will endanger the family!*

The figure in the snow stirred. "Please," he whispered, his voice just a hiss.

I stepped to his side, crouching down to touch his face. His eyes opened a crack, and then...

He looked at me.

I felt hollowed out and filled up again as our gazes collided—mine and this Farther from beyond the edge of my world—and then his eyes shut as he passed out again, and I was released from the spell of them. I stepped back quickly, but the damage was already done. There was already an ache in my chest from the knowledge of what we were about to do.

"Lia?" My sister looked from the Farther's still form to my face.

"All right," I said, angry at my own weakness. "Fine. But we have to hurry. It's almost dark."

She dragged in a quick, relieved breath.

31

"Help me carry him," I said. And there was a dull ringing in my head that was telling me I'd gone mad, because the Farthers were almost as dangerous as the Watchers and almost as dangerous as the condemnation of the village Elders. But I could not stand here and tell my sister that we were going to leave the stranger, this Farther, in the snow to die the same way our parents had died, gutted by some Watcher and left to freeze.

Ivy squatted down in the snow and grabbed his legs. I took hold of his arms. One of his sleeves was slick, and I realized that the snow was dark with blood, not mud.

"He is bleeding," I hissed, and Ivy just nodded. She already knew. Our eyes met over the motionless body, and I counted out loud. "One, two, three—"

We heaved him up, but he was too heavy. "Down, then," I said, panting. "We'll drag him."

The snow had begun to harden, and ice formed a thick shell over the rocks and roots of the forest floor. I hoisted him halfway up so that his legs were dragging, then slipped my cloak off and wrapped it around his chest. I began to pull. He slipped across the top of the snow crust with little resistance as we slogged toward home.

"I didn't mean to go into the woods," Ivy began. She grabbed a corner of my cloak to help me. "But I heard moaning, and I was worried that someone was hurt..."

"Don't talk," I gasped, my words coming out terse because of the exertion. "Save your breath. Just pull."

She shook the hair out of her eyes and didn't say anything else. The Farther's head lolled against his shoulder as we lifted him over a rock and back into the snow. He moaned once but didn't wake. He was so cold beneath my hands that I was astonished he was still alive. His body felt stiff and hard as a corpse.

32

Together we struggled to drag him across the snow. The storm was worsening, and the gray-blue light played tricks on my eyes. I spotted a flicker of movement in the shadows, the rustle of a pine branch. Something slipped through the trees in the distance—a Watcher? But when I looked again, there was only the gathering darkness and the falling snow.

We broke through the trees and into the yard. I gasped in relief at the sight of the farm, solid and square and spilling light from the windows. Behind it the woods formed a grim, dark line, reminding me that we had to hurry.

"Not the house," I said when my sister started toward it.

It wouldn't be safe. I clung to that single thought blindly, stupidly...as if there were any sort of *safe* in what we were doing by taking in this Farther.

Ivy didn't argue. Together, we tugged him to the barn.

The barn was warm and dark and smelled like grass after the sharp assault of icy wind. Ivy shut the door while I struggled to move the Farther to the back of the room, behind the horses' stalls where we kept the hay. I threw my cloak back over my shoulders and slipped both arms under his, half-carrying, half-dragging him. The horses nickered at us as I muscled him past them, all the way to the farthest corner that backed up to the rugged side of the mountain—the farthest corner from me and the farthest from the village too. I put him down on a nest of hay and rubbed my aching arms. As a farm girl, I was stronger than most girls my age. But still, it wasn't easy dragging one hundred and fifty pounds of dead weight.

The light that filtered in was soft and blue, the dimmest illumination of that moment before the sun

33

slipped away completely and the moon rose. It touched his unconscious face and made him look like an angel fallen from the sky.

I wondered if the infection would kill him tonight or if it would take days for him to succumb.

His eyes snapped open, and I jerked back. He turned, his gaze searching the darkness before settling on my face. The irises of his eyes were a deep gray-blue, like the sky before a storm, and a shiver that was only partly fear ran down my spine as they met mine.

"Where am I?" he whispered harshly. His hand darted out and snagged my wrist, pulling me forward. "Who are you?"

Ivy touched my shoulder, and the Father's gaze shifted to her face. He scowled, and I felt her stiffen. His fingers tightened on my wrist, but I pulled away just as he fainted again.

Grabbing Ivy, I dragged her away from him and out into the yard. The cold air shocked me into sudden clarity. What had we done?

"Will he be all right?" my sister asked.

"Go to the house. I want you to stay clear of him. He's dangerous."

"What about his wounds?" My sister wriggled free from my hands and looked back at the barn.

I hesitated, weighing her words. "Get the rags, then," I said, because she was right. "And bring some milk and a blanket, too."

She ran.

When she came back with a quilt, a pitcher of milk, and strips of torn-up old clothes we used for cleaning and stuffing cracks, I crouched beside his unconscious body and ripped his shirt open so I could reach the wound. The fabric tore easily. It was some kind of delicate, silky cloth, completely unsuited to the cold

34

weather and the forest terrain. I tossed it aside and took the wet rag from Ivy.

It was dark in the barn now, the light from the open door fading into blue twilight. I cleaned him up as best as I could, wrapping his shoulder with rags for bandages. I had no medicine to give him, nothing. Ivy hovered at my back, shivering and wincing every time I handed her something bloody.

When I'd finished, I packed straw and the quilt around him. At least he'd be warm tonight. I set the pitcher of milk beside his head.

"Come on," I said. "It is almost dark, and the storm is growing worse. We need to be inside."

Ivy looked ready to protest, but she was frightened, too. I locked the barn door, grabbed her arm, and dragged her back to the house before she could try to argue.

Jonn looked up from the yarn as we came in with our flushed faces and wet hair. He absorbed our condition, his expression transforming from relief to concern. "What happened?"

Ivy looked at me and then away. "We have a visitor in the barn," she said.

My brother's face wrinkled in confusion. "A visitor? Lia, what is she talking about?"

I licked my lips. I wasn't sure how to say it. Might as well be blunt. "Ivy found an injured Farther in the woods and insisted we bring him here. He is in the barn. He is dying, I think."

Jonn was silent. A clock ticked loudly in the stillness.

"A Farther?" he repeated, finally.

"Yes." What else was there to say? If the village Elders found out, we would be severely punished, perhaps even lose the farm. It was as simple and as stark

35

as that. I threw another look of pure fury at Ivy, but she was shaking the snow out of her cloak and didn't see it.

"Pick up the laundry," I said to her. "You've left it all over the house."

She started gathering up the blankets and shirts, and I went into the kitchen and paced. There was an old story in our village lore about a girl who found a baby rock snake and took it in as a pet. When she scooped up the snake to cuddle it, the creature sank its fangs into her arm and killed her.

Sometimes pity was a mistake.

I bit my lip as worry gnawed at me again.

A crack of thunder split the air, and sleet began to pelt the glass like pebbles. I peeked through the window and saw that the world had turned into a wall of white. The storm was here.

I went to the fire. Jonn was bent over the yarn in his lap again, his long fingers winding it into a tight bundle for quota day. Ivy joined me, and we stoked the flames high to drown out the sound of the wind shrieking against the joints of the house. Wrapping a quilt around my waist, I picked up a snarl of fibers and settled in a chair, my fingers twisting the material into long strands of cream-colored yarn. I kept one eye on the door, because a piece of me kept expecting the village Elders to kick it down every time so much as a shingle creaked overhead.

This was a mistake, my mind chanted at me, and I wholeheartedly agreed. But try as I might, I couldn't forget the way I'd felt when I'd looked at him in the woods, and he'd looked at me, and it had been as if I'd never seen another person before.

Surely I was going mad to be thinking such things, especially about a Farther.

After what felt like hours of weaving, Ivy made a sobbing sound and tossed down her yarn. "It's too much," she said, her eyes shiny. "I'm exhausted and cold."

I opened my mouth to reprimand her. But Jonn put down the yarn in his lap and pulled out his flute from beneath his chair. Putting it to his lips, he began to play.

The first few notes shivered in the air. They broke the silence like droplets of water splattering against the hearth.

Ivy's shoulders drooped as she succumbed to the beauty of the music. I kept weaving, but my ears were tuned to the notes. The melody dipped and danced, coaxing us to relax before stirring us to smile. My soul soared along with the song as it reached a crescendo.

This was my brother's greatest strength. This was his true calling.

If only there was a quota for beauty, instead of function.

The song ebbed and fell into silence, and we were left breathing in the lack of it. Jonn wiped his lips, smiled gently at me, and began another.

He knew how much Ivy needed it. How much *I* needed it.

His music revived us like water revived a plant. Slowly, I let myself feel the ache that still throbbed deep inside me at the loss of our parents. Our mother had taught him to play after his accident. Now it was one of the few pieces we had left of her.

When he'd finished, we all breathed. Ivy's eyelids began to close. Jonn leaned back and put the instrument away, picking up his yarn again.

Feeling sorry about my earlier harshness toward my sister, I got her a quilt and tucked it around her thin body. She made soft noises like a kitten, her eyes

37

cracking open for a second to look at me. "Love you," she murmured, and my heart melted a little.

I went back to my place, and Jonn and I worked silently into the night as the storm lashed out, and my baby sister fell asleep.

FOUR

THE WIND WHISPERED through the slits in the shutters and beneath the cracks in the door. Jonn slept, his body curled up like a cat's and his head on his folded arms. Ivy was also asleep, her body leaning against Jonn's chair. I sat before the fireplace, a blanket around my shoulders and my father's pistol in my hand.

Outside, the wind howled and moaned. But as always, I loved the sound of it, because it drowned out the worse sounds.

The screams.

They were inhuman, those sounds—high and keening, like birds of prey. Shivers ran up and down my skin as I listened to the calls that echoed through the night, a horrible song played in time with the fury of the wind, calling and answering each other. These were the sounds *they* made. Watchers. The screams were proof that they existed and not just in my nightmares.

I winced as another shriek tore through the night. Terror dried up my mouth and made my bones feel soft. I burrowed deeper into the blanket and gripped the gun tightly. It was old and didn't work, as far as I knew—I'd never seen my father use it. But holding it made me feel safer, so I cradled it in my lap and counted the seconds.

The Watchers only screamed during storms. Otherwise, they were utterly silent as they crept through the forest.

I thought of the meager row of blossoms dangling over our door and shuddered again as a shrill shriek lacerated the silence before dying off like a wounded animal. All the hairs on my arms prickled. And when the door shuddered as if something was clawing it, I jumped to my feet and lifted the gun. Jonn stirred in his sleep.

I waited, ready to shoot if anything tried to enter. Sweat slid down my back. The wind moaned again, sounding like the injured Farther in the barn. I gritted my teeth and kept the gun pointed at the door, even when my arm began to ache. I stayed standing until the storm calmed in the early hours of the morning. When I finally slumped to the floor in utter exhaustion, I slept.

~

Morning light touched my face, waking me.

"Lia?" It was Jonn's voice.

I sat up with a start, brushing my hair from my face. The room smelled like sweat and ashes. The fire was almost cold, and my nose was chilled. My gaze darted around the room—to the fireplace, where the ashes had grown cold, to the shutters, streaming with sunlight, to the door, still barred shut.

I zeroed in on that last detail, and I felt myself over to be sure I was truly alive and whole. And I was.

"We're all right," I breathed aloud. With every scream-filled storm that came, a part of me feared that we would not be alive in the morning. And every time, the relief was sweet.

The Watchers had left us unscathed.

Jonn watched from his chair as I stood and stretched. Amusement touched his mouth, making him look devilish. "Did you spend the whole night awake and ready as usual?"

40

"No." I did not mention that while I *had* slept, it had only been for a few hours. I did not mention the gun, either.

He smiled his disbelief. He was able to sleep through the storms, his faith in the blossoms' power to keep out the Watchers strong. I was the one who could never shut my eyes for fear that we'd be eaten while we dreamed.

"I slept, Jonn," I said, and my voice was a little sharper.

He raised one eyebrow, annoying me. There was little humor in the situation, although Jonn would milk it for any amusement he could find.

I rolled my eyes. I didn't have time to argue with him. We had quota to meet. We had yarn to spin and bundle into balls, not to mention the animals to tend and the—

The Farther. Anxiety dropped onto my shoulders like a heavy quilt as the memories of the night before swept over me. *The Farther was in our barn.*

I scanned the room. "Where is Ivy?"

Jonn looked at the window without speaking, and I hissed a curse and grabbed my cloak. Shoving open the door, I pounded through the freshly fallen snow for the barn.

~

She was already inside, her back pressed to the door and her eyes wide. I went straight past her for the hay, my heart squeezing tight and my mouth suddenly dry.

Had he died in the night?

His eyes were closed and his face was pale. He was not dead, though—I saw the shallow rise and fall of his

41

chest beneath his strange shirt and coat. Something in me loosened at the confirmation of his survival, like I'd been holding my breath.

Ivy reached my side. "He was moaning," she said. At her words, he made a sound of pure agony that made my heart ache even if he was a dangerous Farther.

"He is probably full of infection." I needed to step closer, to look him over, but I wasn't sure if it was safe. I remembered last night and his expression when he'd woken in the barn. He had not looked grateful.

"His wound..." She pointed at the place where the blood had blackened his torn shirt and arm. "Shouldn't we clean it again?"

I pressed my lips together. There was no way I was letting her within three feet of this Farther, not when he was awake. "Bring me some warm water and soap, and an extra shirt of Jonn's. And some of the stew left over from last night's supper. He's probably hungry now."

She hesitated, wanting to argue. The nervousness I felt rose up in me like a wave, and I snapped, "Go."

She went.

With her gone, I could really examine him in the light of day. Last night it had been too dark to really see anything. His groaning was loud now, almost a keening. I'd heard the sound of my grandfather dying from stomach-sick years ago, and it was much like this. I crept closer, my midsection churning.

He was barely visible under the straw that covered him. His eyelids cracked open when I approached, and he rustled beneath his blanket of hay. I faced him without smiling or cowering. I wanted him to know that I was not afraid of him. Or at least, I wanted him to think that I wasn't.

"You," he whispered. His breath hissed between his teeth as the pain seized him again, and he shuddered.

"You are one of those Snow People, the ones who live in the Frost."

He was young, I supposed, probably not much older than me. But his voice had a strength in it that made him sound older than that. His hair was thick and dark, like every Farther I'd ever seen, and his skin was tanned darker than my pale Frost complexion. He had a thin, sharp face and lashes as long as a girl's. They fluttered as he squinted at me.

"Yes," I said, because the term *Snow People* was accurate enough when describing my village, although that was not what we called ourselves.

He took in my expression, and his eyes narrowed. "What are you going to do to me? Let me die? Or give me back?"

"Give you back?" I asked. What was he babbling about?

He sighed, and I realized that he had passed out again. His face turned the color of gravel and perspiration dotted his forehead.

I moved closer. My skin tingled at my nearness to him. There had been malevolence in his eyes—what if he sprang forward and grabbed me? What if he tried to hurt me? But he was unconscious and sick, and as my fears lessened, I grew bolder and leaned in to study his wound.

The blood had dried, leaving a sticky river of brownish-black down his shoulder and arm. The strange clothing on his back hung in tatters, exposing the torn flesh, and bits of rock and straw studded the wound. I could see from the severity of it that he would be dead before long.

The skin around his wound was swollen. I probed it gently.

43

He jerked awake at my touch, and his eyes flew open as he cried out. I staggered back, startled. Our eyes met.

Sweat ran down his forehead and dripped onto his nose. His eyes were wild with pain and terror.

"Please," he whispered, and for a moment he looked pitiful instead of defiant and dangerous.

I didn't know what he wanted.

Ivy returned, the bucket of soapy water spilling a little as she set it down by my feet. She handed me the bowl of stew and Jonn's shirt. Her eyes widened as she saw he was awake.

The Farther gazed at her with a mixture of anger and detachment, and Ivy stepped back and wrung her hands under his stare. She was good at rescuing things and wretched at doing anything about it afterward. I'd already spent most of the last fourteen years disposing of the animals she'd saved after they died without her knowing. But this stranger in our barn was not a bird with a broken wing. It would take more than a trowel and a soft place under a bush to make this problem go away.

"Eat the stew before you starve," I said.

The Farther picked it up. He ate quickly, hungrily.

"The rag," I commanded Ivy, and she dipped it in the water. Shoving up my sleeves, I crouched beside him and took his shoulder in my hands.

"What are you doing?" he gritted, his voice low and hard. He dropped the empty bowl and tried to rise.

"Lie still," I said. "I'm just cleaning the wound."

"Why?"

What did he mean, *why?* I pressed the rag hard against his skin, and he twitched with pain. "So you won't die from infection," I said, and I used the harshest

44

tone I possessed so he wouldn't know how terrified I was.

He watched me warily, but he didn't move as I took off the old bandage and pressed the rag against the wound. The Farther hissed in agony as the hot water touched his flesh, but he held still while I washed the dried blood away and examined him. The wound was deep, but I saw no infection yet. I rinsed the injury carefully, dabbing at the torn edges of his flesh with the rag. I could feel his muscles beneath my hands, tense and coiled.

As I washed the blood away from the wound, I saw that his shoulder was inflamed as well. Another injury? I prodded the area gently, feeling something hard and flat lodged there, as if the tip of a blade had broken off just below the surface of the skin. What was this? I got my fingers around it and tugged gently, and his hands grabbed at the straw as his face contorted in pain and a moan escaped his mouth.

"That hurts," he gritted through clenched teeth, turning his head to look at me. His eyes captured mine, and his gaze frightened me. The fear in my belly was like a trapped bird, scrambling and fluttering, but I shoved those feelings down because I had to be strong.

"Lie still," I repeated for the third time. I tried to speak firmly, but my voice shook. "Something is buried in your back."

"It hurts—"

"Lie still! Do you want to die from infection?"

That shut him up. His whole body trembled as I touched the injured flesh, but this time he didn't snap or try to pull away. I used the rag to wipe at the place. The rag dislodged a flap of dangling skin that had been torn by whatever had caused the other wound and revealed some of the thing in his back. I pinched it between my

45

fingers and tugged again. Metal glinted against my finger.

I couldn't tell what it was—some kind of metal that had become buried in him. It wasn't a rock or a pebble—too smooth. Whatever it was, it shouldn't be there. I pulled harder, wiggling the piece. It was slippery with blood, and when my fingers found purchase I yanked.

The Farther's head snapped back, and a scream pried its way from his lips. Ivy made a strangled sound and covered her eyes. Sweat broke out across my back.

"Just pull it out," he panted.

I gave a final wrench and pulled it loose, and his whole body stiffened as he fainted against the straw.

"Oh," Ivy said. "Oh."

I sat back hard, my fingers bloody and my skirt wet from where I'd dropped the rag. I was breathing hard, and my muscles were tight. I locked eyes with my sister, and she must have read the murder in my gaze.

"I'll get more clean rags," she murmured, scrambling for the door.

The barn was very quiet now. I turned the thing over in my hands. It was small and square, covered in his blood and etched with lines that might have been a symbol or picture. They meant nothing to me. I wiped the blood on the straw and slipped the metal piece into my pocket before I finished cleaning the wound. Ivy returned with more rags, and I bound up his shoulder with them.

"What do we do now?" she whispered.

I wiped my hands on my skirt and pulled my mother's pocket watch from my skirt pocket. "Now you work your fingers off getting quota filled. I have to go into the village. I cannot miss another Assembly."

"Stupid Assemblies," Ivy muttered.

46

"At last, something we agree on." Smiling wryly, I gathered the rags and stood. "Keep an eye on the barn. I probably shouldn't even have to say this, but don't let anyone inside for any reason." I headed for the door.

"Lia?" she asked, and her voice hitched at the end of my name.

"Yes?"

"What are we going to do with him?"

I just looked at her, because I had no earthly idea. How did she expect me to know?

Her big eyes filled with tears, and I felt myself soften. "It'll be all right, Ivy," I said. "We'll figure something out."

Outside, I leaned against the barn as I examined the results of the storm in the light of day. A few of the fence posts had sagged over or tumbled down, and a loose shingle dangled from the farmhouse like a tooth in the face of a fist fighter. As I was looking, the wind blasted over the trees and swept my cloak into a snarl around my legs. I stooped to set down the heavy bucket so I could rearrange it, and as I bent over I froze at what I saw.

A line of claw prints made a path through the snow, past the barn and around the house. They led into the forest.

I'd only seen a Watcher once in person, when I was a little girl. I was leaving the barn early one morning before dawn after milking the cow, the steaming pail of milk in one hand and a glowing lantern in the other. I realized as soon as I saw the curls of vapor in the freezing air that I'd forgotten the lid, and I left the lantern in the snow as I ran back for it so I'd have a free hand. When I returned, the door creaking beneath my hand, I saw something skitter away from the circle of light, just a flutter of fur and a scrape of metal against

47

metal as it slipped back into the darkness at the edge of the trees. The ice along the path was sliced up as if someone had taken a knife to it. I almost thought I'd imagined it.

But there was no mistaking the tracks, then or now.

Ivy saw them and put her fingers over her mouth. She didn't speak.

"Go back to the house," I said finally. "I need to get into town."

FIVE

THE SKY WAS clean-swept and clear. The air tasted crisp and new. Sunlight sparkled on the fresh-fallen snow, making the trees and branches look encrusted with diamonds. But I couldn't enjoy the beauty. The fear in my stomach was gnawing at me like a rat again. I hurried down the path toward the village. With all the things that had gone wrong in the last day—the Farther, the Watcher tracks, the storm, the almost-missed quota—I couldn't be late to another Assembly, too.

I crossed paths with Adam Brewer close to town, and I swear he looked at me like he knew the secret I kept. Our gazes met briefly, and this time I didn't even make a pretense of greeting him. I just put my head down and pushed on.

At last the town swung into view. Our village huddled against the side of the mountains like a calf seeking protection against its mother, although I found the idea of seeking solace against the mountains ironic, since the stony crags had always been less than forgiving of us. But at least here, we had the hope of safety.

As I approached the familiar stone houses with their sloping moss-covered roofs and sturdy wooden doors painted blue and hung with snow blossoms, my heart thumped in my chest and my mouth grew dry. Could they sense the fear on me? Would they look at me and know what I'd done, what I had hidden in my barn?

My friends stood in a cluster near the door of the Assembly Hall. Ann spotted me and waved, a smile stretching across her face, and for half a second I was tempted to run straight to her and tell her everything that had happened—the Farther, the thing I'd pulled from his back, my stupid sister, the Watcher tracks in the fresh morning snow. All of it. She was my closest friend. She would understand, wouldn't she?

But something held me back, like an invisible hand pressed over my mouth to keep me silent.

"You came," Everiss said, startling me with her sudden nearness at my elbow. She looked as if she'd just come from her family's shop. A smear of blue dye stained her wrist.

"I said I was going to, didn't I?" I meant it to be sassy, but my nerves were fried and my tone came out too sharp. I tensed, waiting for the questions. Waiting for the accusations. They would know...they would suspect...

But Everiss just laughed and hooked her arm into mine, dragging me forward, and my moment of weakness about telling Ann vanished. The group clustered around me, and Cole tipped his head and smiled slyly. I tried to smile back because Ann was giving me her "be sociable" frown, but worry made my lips feel heavy as lead. I grimaced instead.

The others chatted about socials and engagements and making quota. I stood silent, still immobilized by the gnawing rat of worry in my belly.

The bell rang, calling us in. People began to stream from the doors of shops and houses, sweeping us along with them inside the sanctuary. I followed Ann, Everiss, and Cole to one of the hard wooden benches and sat.

A man stepped to the front of the room—Ann's father. He was tall and thin, with a perpetually gaunt face and wide brown eyes topped with bushy eyebrows.

He and Ann had the same nose and mouth, but otherwise she looked like her mother. I saw her smile a little as he waved his hands for everyone's attention.

I settled down as he began by reading the marks. Assemblies were long and boring, and they wasted time—time I could be using to fill my quota or do the necessary chores around the farm, like cooking, caring for the animals, washing laundry, and cleaning the house.

While the names were read aloud, my mind returned to the barn and the Farther we had hidden inside.

Even with his wounds cleaned and bandaged, there was the risk of infection. I chewed my lip as I contemplated what we would do if he died. Or if he lived.

"Lia," Ann hissed. "Are you listening?"

I sighed and sat up a little straighter. I loved Ann, but lately she was vexing me almost as much as Ivy.

The Mayor finished reading the names and and moved on to the community rules, a weekly tradition that grew duller every time I heard it. His voice droned, and my thoughts returned again to the problem currently sleeping in my barn. The Farther. Sweat broke out across my back, and when Ann leaned over and smiled at me, I couldn't smile back.

I was being stupid. No, I was being worse than stupid, I was being reckless. When my parents died, the responsibility for my safety and my siblings' safety had fallen on my shoulders. Even though I was young, the Elders believed I was capable of handling my family's quota and duties, and so they'd allowed us to continue living in the farmhouse instead of splitting us up to go to other families. They'd almost sent Ivy to live with the Washers, who lived above the Mayor's house and spent their days up to their elbows in scalding, lye-filled water.

51

A shudder rippled through me at the thought of my sister trapped in that place. She was the most exasperating creature I'd ever known, but I didn't wish her to be in torment. And spending her days sweating and straining at back-breaking labor while her hands turned puffy and red, never able to feel the sun on her face as she worked, or rescue her stupid animals? It would be a particularly vicious punishment for her.

But now, with the rescued Farther in the barn... If they thought I was incapable of following the rules and meeting the family quota, they would reassign me and take Ivy and Jonn away. Even though he was a man by our standards, Jonn was barely treated better than a child because of his withered leg and poor health. I didn't know what would happen to him.

"All members of the community must fulfill all assigned quotas on time, attend the weekly Assemblies..." The Mayor was still reading the rules aloud. I took a deep breath and let it out. All was not lost yet. I still had time to sort this out. I would think of something.

Beside me, Cole was fidgeting, which made me feel a little better. At least I was not the only person who hated Assemblies.

The Mayor finished the list of rules and moved on to the courtship and marriage lists. Cole shifted as the names were read aloud. He snuck a glance at me, and I pretended not to notice.

When the readings were finished, the Mayor surveyed the crowd. "We have an important matter to discuss," he said.

My heart began to pound, although I knew it was irrational. I had just come from the farm. The barn was undisturbed. We were at the edge of the Frost. No one

52

knew about the Farther in our barn except Jonn, Ivy, and me.

But my palms turned clammy with dread anyway.

"There have been increased reports of Watcher tracks lately."

The room seemed to shrink a little as the word left his lips. Everyone flinched, some muttered. I remembered the tracks across the yard and around the house. Watchers had been in our yard, too. My stomach felt sick and my heart began to beat faster, like a pounding hand against the wall of my chest.

Ann looked at me, her head cocked to one side. I gave her a weak smile, trying to swallow a little of my panic.

"Any member of the community who is out early or late must exercise extreme caution—carry snow blossoms at all times, and be sure to hang them on your doors and windows." He paused, his gaze sweeping the hall, and I swear it lingered a moment on me. "There have been some reports of sightings, even. This boldness is troubling. We do not know what has caused the Watchers to become so active, but we do know that everyone needs to be more careful at this time."

A few of the people around me began whispering. I saw the worried glances, the wide eyes. The Farmers and others who lived on the outskirts of the community looked most unsettled, because they were the ones most likely to encounter one of the creatures.

"Don't be unduly alarmed," the Mayor continued, flashing the crowd a reassuring smile now. "Simply be prepared. Follow the rules and work hard. Safety, fraternity, integrity."

We repeated it after him. *Safety, fraternity, integrity.* It was our village motto and highest code. Because of our

53

high level of organization and our strong set of rules, we'd survived when other communities here had failed.

Guilt stabbed at my heart as I spoke the words, because I had failed the first imperative—safety. I might have failed the last, too, because I was harboring the Farther in my barn and I was keeping him a secret. But I didn't know what else to do—I'd picked up a rock snake, and I was afraid to let it go lest I be bitten and killed.

We were dismissed after repeating the motto. Villagers stood and streamed for the doors, whispering about the Watchers or discussing the courtship lists. I sat in my place, feeling miserable and numb.

Ann grabbed my arm and clung to it tightly, as if she would be safe as long as she hung onto me. "Can you believe the news about the Watchers?"

"It's frightening," I said, trying to keep my voice steady. In my mind's eye I kept seeing the tracks in front of the barn. Sometimes I felt a little resentful of Ann. She lived in the town and the Watchers were just a scary story here. It was the ones who lived on the edges of the village grounds that had to really worry. People like me, people who were already struggling to meet quota and feed their families.

"Will your family be safe?"

"We'll be fine," I murmured. I thought of the Farther in the barn again, and my stomach tightened. Right now, I had worse problems on my mind.

Apparently my lackluster response failed to satisfy her. "Lia," she said, putting her hands on her hips. "Are you all right? You seem...distant."

"I'm just thinking," I replied, standing and giving my skirt a shake. "And I'm really tired. The storm kept me awake last night."

Ann bit her lip, sympathy flashing in her eyes. "You've always hated the storms, haven't you?"

54

Cole, who'd been listening quietly from a few feet away, stepped over and inserted himself into the conversation. "I have a hard time believing you're afraid of anything, Lia."

His smile was wide and sly, like he was paying me a compliment, but I felt only intense irritation. How little he knew me, if he thought that. I was afraid of everything. I had to be, if I wanted my family to survive to the next winter. And sometimes it seemed like I was the only one who worried about these things.

Right now I wanted to be left alone so I could think about them in peace.

Cole saw my expression. His smile faded. Ann saw, and rushed to salvage the mood. She followed me down the aisle toward the door, Cole at her side. "Are you coming to the social?"

She didn't look at Cole when she asked, and I had the sudden suspicion that this conversation had been planned between them.

"I don't know," I said, brusque. "I can't promise anything." I loved her, of course, but at the moment I wanted to be rid of her so I could go home and make sure Ivy and Jonn were alive and well, and the Farther was undiscovered.

"Come on," Ann coaxed, not noticing my impatience or maybe just ignoring it. "There's going to be sweets, and music, and dancing...more fun than we've had in months. Surely you don't want to miss it."

"I won't have anything to wear," I said, both because it was a good excuse and because it was true. Speaking of my poverty usually shut people up.

But Ann was undeterred this time. "Borrow something of mine. We're the same size."

"Come on, Lia," Cole said.

"All right," I said, just so they would leave me alone.

55

Ann beamed. She hugged me, releasing me abruptly when her father called her name. "I have to go—those pillows won't make themselves."

Cole and I were left standing together, watching her saunter off arm in arm with her father. A tiny flicker of exhausted resentment rose in my chest—how was it that her quota involved cross-stitching on decorative pillows, and mine involved hours of spinning yarn?

Cole shuffled his feet and fiddled with his hands. The sly smile crossed his face, but he schooled it into a serious expression. "Lia..."

I looked toward the paths to the farms, anxiety gnawing at me again.

"About the social," he said, and then stopped. "Maybe it's painfully obvious, but..."

Pain. That reminded me. "I need to visit the market," I said.

He paused. "I'll accompany you."

We walked swiftly, me because I was worried about Ivy and Jonn and the farm, him because he was trying to keep up with me. I spotted the woman I needed—old Tamma Gatherer, with her bags of dried herbs and roots. She sold the extras in the market after making her quota every week.

"What herbs would you suggest for a deep wound that might become infected?" I asked when I reached the stall, my voice barely above a whisper. I wished Cole would go away, but he lingered within hearing distance. I silently willed him to not listen, or not ask me questions.

Tamma pursed her lips. "Blood's bane, for the wound, and fever root for the sickness that will come from the infection."

I took the herbs from her outstretched hand. They rustled in my hand as I slid them into my pocket. I

56

withdrew a small bundle of yarn from my other pocket and slipped it to her. My insides ached—that could have gone toward our quota—but the Farther needed medicine if he was going to survive another night.

"One of your horses injured?" she asked, her eyebrow lifting shrewdly. "The cow?"

I flushed. "No." I turned and left before she could ask any more questions. As I walked away, I berated myself for acting so suspicious. I should have chatted, perhaps suggested something that would have given her a different impression.

Cole caught up to me again. A few of the other villagers glanced up at us from their chores with knowing smiles, and my face flushed. Was my reluctant courtship the talk of the whole town?

"You're in such a hurry."

"I have to get back," I said. "Lots of yarn to spin."

"Quota, quota, quota," he growled. "You never talk about anything else."

I bit down on my tongue to keep from snapping at him. "What else is there?" I said, sharply. Between my crippled brother and my airheaded sister, we never had enough hands, it seemed, but I couldn't tell the Elders that or they'd split us up and take the farm.

Cole's eyes narrowed. "Come on, Lia. You'll never get anywhere with that attitude."

I glanced over the herbs Tamma had given me, mentally calculating how long they'd last. *Get anywhere?* As if there was any future for someone in our village besides back-breaking work. "What is that supposed to mean?"

"You wait and see," he said, his voice suddenly fierce. "One day I'm going to be at the very top, and you'll wish you'd believed in me then."

57

I glanced at him, and the intensity in his gaze frightened me a little. "Cole..."

"Sorry," he said, turning his head to hide his gaze a moment. When he looked back, his expression was neutral again, and he smiled at me and changed the subject. "You should come by and see me at the shop sometime," he said. "Next time you're in town for your quota." He emphasized the word with a flick of his eyebrows.

I forced a smile. "I wouldn't want to interrupt your work." With a shrug, I turned to go.

"Lia," he said, grabbing my wrist. "An interruption from you is never a bother."

My eyes dropped to his hand, and I held them there, warning him silently. He blushed and let go. We were *not* courting. He had no right to make advances.

"I'm sorry," he started to say, but I cut him off.

"I must go."

He fell back, and I could feel his eyes boring into my back as I took the path toward the farms.

A shadow detached from the alleyway beside me. Adam Brewer. My heart squeezed into my throat, and I walked faster, but he blocked my path.

Our gazes tangled. I sucked in a breath, and his jaw twitched.

"I need to speak with you," he said.

No greetings, no small talk. Just that. I didn't know what to say.

Adam waited. Wind stirred his hair and ruffled his cloak. The sunlight against the snow around him blinded me, making me blink and turn away. "What do you want?" I gritted. I was tired from dealing with Cole. I was anxious from the news I'd heard at Assembly.

"Your family—they are all well?"

58

The question stung, coming from him. I lifted one shoulder in a shrug. "I suppose."

"Your farm is far from the rest of the village," he said. He seemed to be choosing his words carefully. Was he trying to antagonize me, or was this his clumsy attempt at making friends? "Do you see much out there?"

See much? I hesitated, thinking of the Farther. Did he suspect...?

No. None of them could possibly know. I was being too nervous, too jumpy.

"Not much," I said.

Adam glanced over my head at the forest beyond the village walls. "The woods can be lonely on the farms. Ours is quite remote too. Nothing but ice and trees all around."

"Yes," I agreed. Was he trying to tease a confession from me, or establish solidarity? This conversation was turning into a deadly dance.

Adam hesitated. I could see him weighing the words in his mind. "The Watchers don't wander too close?"

A shiver of anger went through me, and I turned my head to stare into his face without responding.

He flinched at my expression. "I know certain accusations have been made against my family—"

I almost choked. "Accusations?"

His eyes narrowed. "Yes. Accusations."

I couldn't contain the words that burst out of me. They burned on my tongue, hot with fury. "Calling them accusations implies that you feel they are not true. My parents are *dead*, Adam. Dead! That has not been fabricated. And they were helping your father with his quota when it happened. He left them in the forest alone with his barrels while he went back for more. He didn't report them missing to the Elders. Can you deny it?"

He hesitated. Was it guilt that kept him from spitting the words out? Did he want to apologize for my parents' deaths?

"I cannot."

My hands formed fists. Nervous energy danced over my skin, fueling my words. "Leave me alone. Don't try to be my friend."

"Your parents—"

"*Don't* speak to me about my parents," I said, shutting my eyes. "I'm sick of this conversation."

Whirling, I headed for the gate, and home.

He didn't follow.

SIX

MY ANGER HAD settled into a cool resolve by the time I reached the farm again. I shut Adam Brewer and his baffling behavior from my mind as I stared down at the house from my vantage point at the top of the hill. I couldn't worry about him right now. I had more than enough on my proverbial plate already. I needed to ensure we made quota, and I needed to deal with this Farther in our barn. I went down into the yard, heading for the house.

A cold wind blew down from the mountains, chilling my cheeks and stealing my breath. I inhaled deeply, my hand on the door, and then I went inside.

Jonn looked up from his place by the fire. Ivy sat beside him, her hands full of yarn, and I almost slumped against the wall with relief that she hadn't run off again.

"Took you long enough," she said, glaring.

"I had to get herbs for your Farther..."

"He's not *my* Farther," Ivy said.

"...And then Cole Carver wouldn't leave me alone." I didn't mention Adam Brewer.

"Cole Carver?" Jonn looked amused.

"Bringing him home was your idea," I said to Ivy, shooting Jonn a warning look. Unperturbed by my glare, he grinned.

I went into the kitchen and fetched a kettle. Filling it with water from the pump, I stomped to the fireplace and slung it over the cooking spit.

61

"What did they say in Assembly?" Jonn asked.

"The usual. Rules, rules, don't break the rules. No mention of Farthers. But the Watchers have been sighted in greater numbers lately." A chill slipped down my spine just saying it. "I saw some of their tracks this morning in the yard."

Ivy paled. Jonn straightened, the blanket around his waist slipping over his knees. "Do they know why the Watchers are acting restless?"

I shook my head. I already had a sick stomach just thinking about those tracks in the snow. "They said they didn't. They said to keep wearing the snow blossoms and to be careful after dark." My eyes moved to the yarn. "How's the quota coming today?"

He held up a bundle, neatly tied and ready for the sack. A little of the tension drained from my body. It was progress. At least Ivy hadn't wandered off today. Maybe the whole Farther thing was scaring a little sense into her.

I tucked my hand in my pocket, and my fingers brushed metal. The thing from the Farther's back. I pulled it out and held it aloft. Firelight flashed over the slick surface as I turned it.

"What is that?" Jonn asked, leaning forward with interest.

"I took it out of the Farther's back. Do you think it's some sort of bullet?"

"Hmmm," he said. I put it into his fingers, and he turned it over. "It's a shoddy bullet if that's what it is. The shape is all wrong. And what are these etchings?"

I took it back from him and put it in my pocket. Maybe I would ask the Farther himself.

When the water in the kettle heated, I poured it into a bucket and headed for the door with the bucket in one hand and a packed basket of food for his dinner in the other. I had to get this out of the way before nightfall. Hopefully he was well enough to swallow some dry bread and cheese, because I had little else.

"Shall I come with you?" Ivy asked.

"No, work on the weaving." With the herbs in my pocket and the bucket and basket in my arms, I slipped to the barn and struggled to get the heavy door open with my arms full. I let the bar fall down behind me as I stepped inside and crept toward the nest of hay in the back.

He was covered so thoroughly that I couldn't even see him. He must be getting cold. Outside, the wind howled as if to punctuate my thoughts. I set down the bucket and the food and stepped forward—

He came out of nowhere, hitting me hard from one side and knocking me over. We rolled together across the floor and he came out on top, his hands on either side of my head, holding my wrists down against the stones. His burning eyes bored into mine.

I couldn't seem to find my breath. The whole world slowed down, and I realized with perfect clarity that he might kill me.

"Don't scream," he hissed.

I shook my head.

"How far is the village?" He whispered it, the words harsh and raspy in the air between us. I could see his mind working behind his eyes—was he calculating how long it would take him to try to struggle away on his own, how long before they found my lifeless body?

I was neither brave nor stupid. I told him what he wanted to know. "The village is less than a mile."

He grimaced, and I realized he must be half-mad with the pain. Maybe if I moved suddenly, I could throw him off and get to the door...

63

He must have sensed my plan, for he pressed down harder on my wrists, keeping me pinned. "And the gate?"

"What gate? You mean the village gate?"

He didn't explain. "The mountains, then."

"The farm sits in its shadow," I gasped. His hands were cutting off my circulation. "But killing me does nothing to help you. You are too weak to get far, and the Watchers fill the woods."

His eyebrows drew together sharply, and he coughed. He was weakening—I could see it. "Kill you?"

His grip on my wrists slackened. I saw my chance, and I took advantage of it.

I slammed my elbow into his face. The Farther cried out, falling sideways like a puppet with its strings cut. I scrambled up for the door and yanked it open.

"Stop—wait—"

I turned. He was crumpled on the ground, his limbs shaking. I could see that he had no strength left.

"I'm sorry if I hurt you," he gasped. "I just needed answers."

I lingered, not running but not relaxing, either. "You would kill me for information, then?"

He pressed a hand against his side and wheezed a bewildered laugh. "I'm not a murderer of farm girls. Not even those who plan to harm me."

"Harm you?" My words were sharp. "I'm sticking my neck out for you. I'm putting my family in danger for you. I'm sheltering and feeding you—and for what? It's you who just tried to harm me."

"I just needed information about my location," he said, wincing at my words. He struggled up into a kneeling position and raised his dazzling blue eyes to mine. Blood colored his lip red. "I won't try anything again, I promise, even though I know you want me dead."

64

It was my turn to laugh, breathlessly. "You make no sense." I grabbed the herbs from my pocket and brandished them at him. "I came to bring you these for your wound. I'm not going to kill you. I just want you gone before you can cause any more trouble."

His expression turned inside out—the planes of his face softened in surprise, and his eyes widened slightly. But then they slitted shut, and I could tell he didn't believe me. "You're lying."

"Why would I lie?" I snapped. "If I wanted to kill you, I'd have done it by now. I could have simply left you in the snow, or refused to clean your wounds, or refused to feed you."

He was silent, considering this. Some of the wild terror on his face eased at the logic of what I'd said. "Why haven't you? Left me to die, I mean?"

I didn't answer that, because I didn't know how to put my reasons into words. I didn't even quite know what the reasons were.

But he was waiting for an answer.

"We had a dog, once," I said slowly.

The Farther licked his lower lip where it was bleeding from my assault. He was listening.

"It was a pitiful little thing with half a tail and button-black eyes. It chased the chickens and made a nuisance of itself, and once it got lost in the forest and we couldn't find it. Eventually it came back with one leg dragging. It was shivering and sick. We don't have time to take care of sick pets, you know, but...my mother nursed that little thing back from the brink of death. I asked her why, and she said life was precious. She said we couldn't forget that."

"Did it live?" he asked, softly.

"She," I muttered. "I remember—it was a female. Snowball. And she lived. She died of old age last winter."

65

Fresh blood was blooming across his shoulder beneath the bandage. I stepped forward and found the bucket again. "Take off your shirt."

He lifted his eyes to mine, startled.

"I've just told you—I'm not letting you die. You're weak with fever, and I need to tend to that wound. Take off your shirt."

He slid it over his head without a word, bracing himself in a half-kneeling position while I examined the wound. It looked bad. The skin was puffy and inflamed, and blood and puss had seeped into the bandages. But I could fix this.

I mixed the herbs with the hot water and then dipped the rags into them. "This will help," I said, pressing them against his back a little too hard because I was mad at him for trying to attack me. I put one hand against his shoulder as I worked, and it was hot with fever. When I'd finished, his arms were trembling with the effort of staying upright. I picked up the rags and tossed his shirt over him, and he collapsed against the straw.

"There's food in the basket for you," I told him. "I'll bring you more in the morning. Stew, if we have it."

I'd gathered up the dirty rags and was turning to go when his voice stopped me.

"I'm sorry. For—for jumping you like that. I thought you wanted to hurt me."

I didn't turn around, but I didn't leave, either. Silence filled the barn.

"What's your name?" he asked.

It was such a quiet question, spoken so hesitantly. I looked down at my shoes, damp from the snow that had fallen off my cloak and begun to melt on the straw. "Lia."

"Lia," he said, like he was testing it out on his tongue. "My family called me Gabe."

I didn't want to know his name. I didn't want that kind of contraband information in my head. But there it—and he—was.

I left, the rags clenched in my hand, and I locked the door behind me.

~

I didn't tell Jonn and Ivy about the incident in the barn, or what the Farther had said. I plunked myself by the fire and worked the spinning wheel with vicious energy, my lips pressed together tightly. My siblings took one look at my expression and wisely refrained from speaking to me. And so the afternoon passed into golden evening, and the evening into darkness, all in silence. We worked steadily at the spinning and binding, and even Ivy was quiet.

My thoughts kept churning, turning the conversation with Gabe over and over in an effort to see every nook and cranny of his words and their meaning. I kept seeing his face when I'd chosen to change his bandage instead of leave—the surprise, then the softness. And a softness lingered in me, too, and I didn't know how to define it.

I thought about the Assembly, and what they'd said about the Watchers. Whenever I thought about the tracks I'd seen in the snow, my throat felt tight and my fingers grew damp. Maybe I should go back into town tomorrow and report the Watcher tracks. It might be relevant for some reason—perhaps there was a pattern to their movements, a predictability that could save someone's life. Maybe someone else wouldn't have to be orphaned the way we were.

Another thought occurred to me suddenly, like a door thrown open. Ann's father. The Farther. If I went to him personally, told him what had happened...

He would understand, wouldn't he? The Elders might be stern and strict, but Ann was my best friend, and I'd known her family since I was a little girl. I would simply go to him and explain everything. Surely he couldn't be too angry with us for trying to help someone in trouble. I knew it might look bad, since Gabe was a Farther, but surely he could figure something out.

It was settled, then. I would go tomorrow and speak to the Mayor.

The hope in my chest was tentative, but it was there, and it warmed me.

Darkness came. The snow fell in a whispering deluge outside the shutters. I wrapped myself in one of my grandmother's star quilts and huddled by the fire, a bundle of yarn to twist up neat in my lap. I listened to the wet silence of the snow—like feathers piling upon feathers, muffling out all the sound, wrapping the house in a hushed and fearful silence. My ears were straining for the scrape of Watcher claws on the step, or the creak of the door, but I heard nothing.

Ivy heaved a sigh from her place beside me. "My eyes are stinging and we've made loads of yarn already. Can we stop now?"

"Are we finished?" I asked, sounding exactly like my mother. But what could I do? She'd been right all those years when she'd pushed our noses against the grindstone.

My sister thrust her lip out in a pout. "I don't think it's fair that you get to go into the village all the time and flirt with Cole while I'm stuck here working."

My hands, stretched out to hand my finished yarn to Jonn, froze in midair. I swiveled to look at her. "What did you say?"

She squeezed her fingers around the yarn in her lap, defiant. "*Flirting.* With *Cole.*"

"What a despicable accusation," I said, feeling my eyes narrow. "I detest Cole."

"He's your friend, isn't he?"

It was a good point. He was a member of my social circle, although I decided then and there that the word *friend* had become a little too diluted if it could truthfully be applied to our uneasy and tension-filled relationship.

"Well, I detest the idea of flirting with him!" I snapped.

But Ivy sensed victory from my defensiveness and pressed on. "I heard Everiss Dyer's mother saying that you'd better marry him quick before he discovers what a sour temper you have. Otherwise you'll just be a dried up husk without a husband for the rest of—"

I made a noise like an angry bear that had been awakened from hibernation and taunted by ugly children. I tossed aside the rest of the yarn and grabbed my sister by both shoulders, shaking her. The air in the room turned hot, Jonn looked like he might be struggling not to laugh, and Ivy faced me like she was being condemned to burn at the stake for something extremely noble—which made her gossip-reporting all the more infuriating.

"I do not have a sour temper—"

"Let go—"

"Don't you think you're proving her point?" Jonn suggested.

We both paused to look at him, panting.

And then, dimly in the distance, we heard screaming.

69

It was faint at first, like a waking dream, but as I dropped Ivy's arms and went to the window, it grew louder.

It was coming from the barn.

This wasn't a Watcher's cry. This scream was lower, throatier. Human.

The Farther.

The argument was forgotten as terror glowed white-hot in my veins. I fumbled for my cloak and the branch of dried snow blossoms that I kept by the stoop. I ripped the door open and stepped out into the breath-stealing cold.

Ivy followed, whimpering. "What are you going to do, Lia?"

The barnyard was an empty expanse of white. I could see the barn through the falling snow—no footsteps, claw marks or otherwise, led to the door. Then I heard Gabe's scream again, muffled but still distinct in the silence of the night.

He must be delirious with fever.

"Fever?" Ivy repeated, and I realized I'd spoken aloud.

That thought was followed immediately by another realization, a worse one.

What if the Watchers heard him?

I didn't know if snow blossoms and blue ribbons would keep them out, not if they wanted to get inside. They stayed away from the village, but we couldn't tempt them, not out here so close to the forest. He needed to be quiet during the night. We all did.

"What should we do?" my sister whispered.

"Stay here." I was already going, before I got too frightened and changed my mind.

The barn was only a few dozen yards from the farmhouse, but the journey seemed to take a lifetime. My breathing was loud and harsh in my ears, the air was cold as death in my lungs, and my heart pounded against my chest like a fist. I reached the door and slid it open. Gabe was sitting up, his face flushed and his eyes glassy. He panted, looking at me without seeing me.

"You need to be quiet," I hissed, reaching him. "It's not safe. The Watchers will hear you."

He whimpered like a child, delirious. He was babbling nonsense. "They've come for me, Lakin," he said to me, desperation coloring his voice. "They've taken me, it's all over now—"

"Shhhh." I put my cold hands against his face, and he melted against them, his eyes fluttering shut with relief. I made a quick, heart-twisting decision. "I'm bringing you into the house."

As soon as I said it I knew it had to happen. He would not continue to survive in the barn, not in this freezing cold while running a fever and crying out from delirious dreams in the night.

"They'll kill me," he gasped. "Lakin, I'm sorry. I know I promised you, but I couldn't help it. I couldn't do nothing."

"Shhhh," I tried again.

"No," he insisted. "I'm trying to tell you—"

"Gabe," I said, speaking his name firmly, and he quieted at the sound of my voice. As I struggled to lift him into a standing position, I wondered who Lakin was. A friend? A sweetheart? A family member?

He sagged against me, his arm around my shoulders and his nose pressed into my hair. "Lakin," he murmured against my neck, and a shiver slipped down my spine. Sweetheart, then. I helped him toward the door.

At least we would leave no suspicious footprints. The snow was falling so steadily that it would fill the holes we left in a matter of minutes. I looked at Gabe,

71

and he seemed lucid now that the icy air was fanning his face. He squinted at the house and then at me.

"Lia?" He sounded confused, pained. Grateful. Something in my stomach twisted painfully. It might have been pity for him. It might have just been nervousness about the Watchers.

"I'm taking you to the house," I said. "Are you ready?" My breath made a puff of cloud in the cold.

He nodded. Worry chased across his face and was gone, replaced by grim determination. "Ready."

For a few breathless moments, we were partners instead of near strangers as we performed a strange sort of three-legged race, staggering across the dark yard. Snow brushed our faces like little cold butterflies and settled across our hair and shoulders. My back prickled with terror the whole way, and with each step I expected a Watcher to appear from the blackness, a phantom in the swirling white poised to take us and leave red splashed across the snow.

But they never came. We reached the house unscathed and unseen. Ivy wrenched the door open, her mouth in the shape of an O. Jonn dropped the yarn when he saw us.

I made it to the fire before my arms gave out. The Farther hit the floor with a groan and looked up. Snow was melting on his eyelashes and the hair that hung into his eyes was wet. Two spots of bright red glowed on his cheeks.

"Thank you," he breathed, before the fever began to take him again.

Ivy grabbed some quilts for him.

I went to close the door.

Outside, something stirred in the darkness, and my heart stuttered as I reached for the snow blossoms.

But it was just a fox. The creature looked at me with wild, unreadable eyes, and I looked back, and then it slipped into the night while I shut and barred the door and returned to the dying boy at my fireside.

The Farther's fever worsened. He rambled about soldiers and prison cells while his sweat soaked into his hair and his cheeks grew hotter and hotter. He whispered and yelled, muttered and moaned. Ivy sat by him, and when he cried she flinched as if he were personally insulting her.

"Please," the Farther begged, grabbing for her hand during one particularly brutal round of fever-induced delusions. "Please don't, please don't."

"What do you want?" she asked, biting her lip. We'd found that talking to him tended to help.

He hesitated. His eyes blinked open, and they swam with tears of pain. "Please don't kill them," he mumbled. "Kill me if you must, but please don't hurt them."

I was stricken by his words, by the pain on his face.

"Please!" he shrieked, and Ivy put her hands over her mouth.

"Gabe." I grabbed his fingers in mine and squeezed tight. They were hot and dry. "You're safe now. Go to sleep."

His eyelids drooped. He looked down at our hands, clasped tight across the quilt. "Don't let go," he mumbled.

"I won't," I said.

And as long as I held his hand, he slept.

73

SEVEN

IN THE MORNING, I put on my nicest dress—a long blue one with white flowers embroidered across the skirt and sleeves—and braided my hair into the traditional thick rope of hair that most Frost women wore. I tucked a few dried snow blossoms into the braid and then stared at my reflection in the dusty mirror that sat propped against the rafters in the farmhouse loft. If I was going to see the Mayor, I needed to look exceptionally presentable, so he wouldn't doubt my capabilities when it came to providing for my siblings. Especially if I was going to confess to breaking a major community rule.

When I descended the rickety ramble of steps that passed for a staircase, I saw the Farther sitting up by the fire, his fever gone and his hair in a snarl. His eyes were completely clear for the first time, and he had a bemused expression on his face, almost a smile. It softened the sharp angles of his face and made him look less threatening. And he was handsome, but in a quiet, intelligent kind of way, like he was used to working inside with old records and books instead of in the fields.

I immediately hated myself for thinking he was handsome, but my rebellious brain continued to think so anyway. I also could not help but admire his uninjured arm, which was visible where the blanket had fallen away. It was surprisingly muscled, given his lean frame.

His eyes swept the room as if he'd never seen anything like it before, his gaze lingering on ordinary and ugly things like the spinning wheel and the pot over the fire. "Are you done ogling me yet?" he asked, smirking, without turning his head to look at me. I wanted him to look—I wondered if he would scrutinize me the way he'd looked at the spinning wheel, an ordinary thing turned strange and wonderful in his eyes, and then my cheeks flushed at the notion. Or maybe that was just because he'd caught me looking in the first place. It was hard to be sure, because my emotions were in such a tangle lately.

I descended the rest of the staircase with what was left of my dignity, pretending indifference. "I wasn't ogling you," I said. I didn't have any evidence to offer to the contrary, though, so I changed the subject. "Your fever broke?"

"I suppose so, since I am lucid and feeling better. Or maybe I have died, and this is the afterlife. Although you and your sister make a pair of strange angels."

I spotted a used teacup and a plate with crumbs on it next to his nest of quilts, and I deduced that Ivy must have fixed him breakfast. That probably explained some of his shockingly high spirits. Food made everyone a little more cheerful.

I took in the rest of the room. Jonn was asleep in his chair, and Ivy was absent as usual. We were functionally alone, and that made me uneasy. But not because I feared he would try to attack me—I couldn't put my finger on why, exactly, but the sensations simmered just under my skin and made my stomach curl.

"You look all dressed up," Gabe—no, the Farther—said as he finally looked at me. "Are you going somewhere?"

75

Going into the kitchen, I took out the bread and cut off a piece. I ate it quickly, without butter or jam. I didn't have time. "I have to go into the village to speak with the Mayor."

The tenor of his voice changed suddenly. "Why?"

I returned to the main room and leaned against the doorway, watching him. "Because I need to figure out what to do with you."

He blinked. I didn't miss the concern that flashed in his eyes. "But your sister said—"

"What did she say?"

He pressed his mouth into a flat line and refused to answer. I scowled. No wonder he'd been so cheerful, if Ivy had been promising him all kinds of impossible things. I couldn't promise him anything, because I didn't know what the Mayor would do, but I knew he didn't need to worry.

"It's going to be all right," I said. "You're going to have to trust me."

Why did the words in my mouth taste like lies?

His eyes followed me to the door, where I gave him one last look and then I slammed it shut behind me.

~

When I left the house, Ivy was exiting the barn. Her steps slowed as I approached, and her mouth pinched in a frown as she caught a glimpse of my face. I grabbed her arm, and her eyes widened.

"What have you been telling the Farther?" I demanded.

"He doesn't want any trouble, Lia. He just wants to get to some gate." She tried to wriggle away, but I wouldn't let her.

76

"A...a what?" What in a thousand frozen winters was she talking about?

"A gate," Ivy insisted.

"To the village?"

"No. He told me about it this morning when I made him breakfast. He's in trouble with the other Farthers, and he's trying to get to safety, but he has to get through the Frost and to this gate first. He said it will take him to safety. He doesn't want to hurt us, or the village. He just needs our help getting there, and then he'll leave."

I dropped her arm as I remembered that he'd asked me the same question when he'd pinned me to the floor. But this was nonsense. A gate to where? The frozen tundra? I'd lived my whole life here in Frost, and never heard of such a thing, and besides—it didn't make any sense. There was nothing above us but icecaps and Watchers. "Do your chores, work on the quota, and don't let the Farther fill your head with stories. And don't promise him anything, Ivy. I don't want you getting even more mixed up in this than you already are."

Not like me, I thought.

I stormed toward the path to the village, kicking up snow.

~

The Mayor's house was in the center of the village. It crowned the top of a hill, so it was visible above all the roofs of the other houses. The house itself was tall and narrow and painted bright white with gray trim, and windows of precious stained glass and a large, wrap-around porch lined with rocking chairs accentuated the aura of wealth it exuded. There was no other house half so fine in the whole village. Even the grounds were opulent, the obligatory snow blossoms planted in swirling patterns by the Gardener family.

I stood at the bottom of the steps and looked up, the anxiety rat gnawing at my stomach again.

What would he say? What would he do to the Farther?

I took a deep breath and let it out. The rush of cold air to my lungs was bracing, and I straightened my shoulders and stared up the steps. I could do this. It was Ann's father, and he would help me.

My mittened hands made a dull thudding sound against the door. I noticed the shiny brass knocker and tried it. I felt very shabby, standing on that massive porch with my ragged blue cloak on my back and wilting blossoms in my hair.

Only a few people moved about in the streets below. Everyone was probably working on filling their quotas, or else avoiding being out for fear of the Watchers.

Footsteps echoed inside the house, and the door was yanked open. A woman wearing a pressed white apron regarded me with suspicion in her flat gray eyes. "If you've brought the pastries quota, you'll have to deliver it around back."

Pastries quota? Our sugar was rationed because of the winter. Why did the Mayor family get pastries? I shook my head. "No—I'm here to see the Mayor."

She squinted at me. "Name?"

"Lia Weaver."

At the mention of *Weaver*, which obviously marked me as a worker instead of one of the Elder family's daughters, the maid began to close the door. "Wait," I said, stepping forward and shoving my foot in the crack before she could shut me out completely. "I'm a friend of Ann's. She'll be furious if she hears I was denied entrance."

It was a gamble—I had never been to Ann's house before, invited or otherwise. But the maid might listen.

She frowned and glanced me over again through the crack. "Come in," she said. "I will ask him. But I make no promises."

With a sigh of relief, I stepped inside. The maid shut the door behind me.

"Wait here," she ordered with a sniff, and disappeared down the hall.

I looked around. The wood floor beneath my feet was shiny with wax. A gleaming brass lamp hung over my head. Rose-painted paper covered the walls, and through a doorway I glimpsed plush furniture and a thick fur rug. Ann's clothing was always a little nicer than the rest of ours, but she never said anything about the luxury that her family lived in. A servant? Special quotas delivered straight to her house? Shining floors and papered walls?

The maid reappeared, and although her frown hadn't been replaced with a smile, she no longer looked at me as though I were dirt on the floor. "He will see you in his study," she said.

We went up a flight of stairs. I was still struggling to keep my mouth from gaping open like a fool's as I stared at the things around me—rugs on the hall floors. A painting on the wall of Ann and her family. More lamps, all shiny brass.

The maid stopped in front of a closed door and knocked gently. I heard the Mayor's low tenor murmuring on the other side. I could just barely make out the words.

"...Eloisa and Aaron...yes, that might be problematic..."

Eloisa and Aaron? My parents' names?

79

The maid knocked again, and the murmuring ceased. "Come in," the Mayor called in a louder voice, and she opened it and moved aside for me.

My heart hammering, I stepped into the room.

EIGHT

HE SAT AT a desk, surrounded by walls of books. A fireplace warmed the room, and through a window white with frost I saw the gate to the village, the path that led to my farm, crowded on both sides with trees, and above the trees, the mountains. The Mayor smiled at me, but I was still hearing my parents' names spoken in his voice, and the gnawing nervousness in my stomach did not ease.

"Sit down, Lia," he said.

I was surprised he knew my name, and it must have showed on my face, because he said, "I knew your parents, my dear. Wonderful folk. So sorry about what happened to them."

"Thank you," I murmured, sinking into a chair looking down at my hands. Coldness seeped through my veins, and every single bit of me wanted to ask him what he'd been saying about them just a moment earlier. But I didn't ask. "They are missed," I said instead.

"Yes," he agreed. "Now, what can I do for you? I do not normally grant audiences with whoever comes to visit me, but you are Ann's friend." He smiled, and his teeth were as bright white as the outside of the house.

I licked my lips, which had become bone-dry. "There is something I wanted to speak with you about, sir."

He raised one eyebrow. "Oh? Please continue."

81

Suddenly I saw Ivy and Jonn in my mind's eye, and my nerve failed. What if he decided I wasn't fit to be in charge of them? What if he split us up and took away the farm?

The Mayor was waiting.

"I...well..."

Sweat formed on my upper lip. What if this was a mistake? Maybe I should have listened to the Farther, spoken to him in more depth. I remembered the way he'd screamed for mercy in his fever-fed delirium, and I squeezed my hands together in my lap. My heart thumped hard, and the words felt too heavy on my tongue.

"What I mean is..."

I remembered him begging as if he was being tortured.

What if they hurt him?

No, no, no—

"What I mean is that I saw Watcher tracks in our yard, in front of the barn."

And then I could breathe again. I hadn't told him. I felt myself deflate, and I sank back in the chair, wondering if I were a coward.

"More tracks?" He sighed and picked up his pen, making a note of it on a map spread across his desk. I leaned forward and glanced at it. There was our village, a large square in the center. There were the farms, spread around the village like unfurled skirts around a girl's waist. There were the mountains of the Frost, and a funny symbol in the corner that looked a little like a flower—

And there, at the edge of the map, was a smudged scrawl. I tipped my head to read it better.

Echlos.

Strange. I'd never heard of such a place before.

82

The Mayor noticed me looked and casually brushed a few of his other papers over the map. "Was there anything else you needed?"

"No," I said faintly, my head swimming as I struggled to make sense of what I'd seen. "I mean, yes. The Farthers..." I put my hand into my pocket, my fingers brushing the metal bit that I'd put there, and I broke off.

"Farthers?" he repeated.

Suddenly the air in the room was too thin, too cold. I struggled to breathe.

The Mayor hesitated. "One more thing, Lia. You're a smart, good girl and I know I can trust you with this information."

My mouth grew dry as I waited for him to continue.

"There is rumor of a Farther in the Frost. A criminal."

"A...criminal?" I whispered.

He could only mean Gabe. I knew it at once, and I felt like I'd been submerged in ice water.

"Yes. He is roaming the Frost in search of money to steal or children to kidnap. He's armed and dangerous, and he could kill you on sight. If you see or hear anything, you be sure to report it to me right away."

I just nodded. My stomach was sick. Half of me was screaming to tell him, and the other half was screaming for me to keep silent. He'd just flat-out told me to tell him about the Farther, and yet...the story was all wrong. Gabe wasn't armed. He wasn't acting like a thief. He was injured, frightened.

He was acting like a fugitive.

Something was wrong here.

"How did you hear about this criminal?" I asked.

The Mayor's gaze sharpened. He didn't answer for a long moment, and sweat broke out across my back as he sat there and looked at me.

83

"How is your family?" he asked at last, instead of replying to my question. "Your sister, your brother—they are in good health?"

I recognized the threat for what it was. I was not supposed to ask questions.

"They are doing well," I said, and thankfully my voice came out even. Maybe too even.

He lifted one eyebrow. "Good."

I sat there. He was still for a long moment, holding me prisoner with his gaze, and then he smiled ever so slightly and folded his hands.

"Is there anything else you needed, Lia?"

I shook my head. I kept my mouth shut because I was afraid what I'd say if I didn't.

"Hilda can see you out, then." He rang a bell, and the maid reappeared.

I followed her to the door, my feet dragging and my mind swirling.

What had just happened in there? Had he *threatened* me?

"Lia!"

I turned just in time to be assaulted by a whirl of arm, bows, and skirts. Ann hugged me tight, whispering in my ear. "What are you doing here?"

"I had to speak to your father," I said. I'd forgotten I might see her here. It was her house, after all.

"My father? Whatever for, you silly goose?"

"Nothing important," I hedged, but she was already talking over me.

"Well, it's perfect timing. You can try on that dress for the social that I promised you could borrow."

"Oh—"

She grabbed my hand and dragged me down the hall to her bedroom, and my mouth dropped open for what seemed like the twentieth time that day as I took it

84

in. She had a bed that would sleep five people, piled with blankets and fluffy pillows. Lacy curtains framed a giant window of yellow and green stained glass. A chandelier sparkled over her dresser, which was crowded with ribbons and powders.

"Here it is," she said, going to the closet and pulling a lace-covered confection.

"I, uh, oh." I was halfway to speechless. The terror of the interview with her father fell away momentarily as I gazed at what she offered me.

The dress was soft blue, the color of snow blossoms and clear skies. Glass beads winked like jewels at the neckline and waist. A wide satin sash cinched the waist.

"What do you think?" Ann held it up to herself to demonstrate the length. She smoothed a hand over the lace and then grinned at me. "It's beautiful, isn't it?"

"I can't believe you're not wearing it," I said. She wanted to let me borrow this beautiful thing?

Ann shook her head, her long curls rustling over her shoulders with the graceful movement. "No, I wore it a month ago at—" She hesitated, biting her lip. She looked away from me as she spoke. "I wore it at a party."

I wondered why she'd stopped herself from telling me where she'd worn it. Did she think my feelings would be hurt because I hadn't been invited? But Ann was already talking again. "Don't worry about me. I'm wearing my newest dress. It's going to go perfectly with my new hair ribbons, look..."

Her dress was beautiful, of course, although I preferred the blue one. I drifted over and let my fingers slide across the fabric while she chattered about how she planned to style her hair.

My thoughts returned to what I'd overheard her father saying while I stood outside his office. Why had he been talking about my parents? Who had he been

85

speaking to? The room had been empty when I'd entered.

Ann was looking at me with her eyebrows raised. She must have asked a question.

"I'm sorry, Ann. My mind was wandering." Guilt swept over me as I admitted it. I was a bad friend—feeling suspicious of her father, not listening to her when she talked. And she was letting me borrow a dress, too. Heat flooded my cheeks.

"It's fine," Ann said, smiling with just the corners of her mouth. "I just asked if you were all right with all the talk of Watchers. Your house is so far out from the rest of the village..."

I gave in and finally told her about the tracks I'd seen. Her mouth formed a perfect O as she listened, and she put her hands to her cheeks.

When I'd finished, she sighed. "I would have died of fright. Lia Weaver, you are the bravest person I know."

Not really brave, I realized, so much as desperate. See, you can't be quite as scared when you have no other choice, because there's nothing between you and the worst except your own stubborn tenacity. But I just shrugged. Ann was my friend and had been so since our days in the village schoolhouse, but there were things we didn't say to each other. The difference in our life situations was one of those things.

"Anyway," Ann said, "let me just wrap this up so you can take it with you."

"Thanks, Ann," I said, and I really meant it.

She looked at me, hesitating, and I got the impression she wanted to tell me something. The silence stretched too long between us, turning awkward, and we both fumbled for something to say.

"I'll see you at Assembly," Ann said finally, with a quirk of her eyebrows that clearly said *come to Assembly.*

And I laughed, because that was Ann—always getting onto everyone and making sure they dotted their i's and crossed their t's.

"I'll be there," I promised her, meaning it.

She smiled, but the smile didn't quite reach her eyes.

When I left the Mayor's house, I went straight to the creek at the edge of the village and tossed the bit of metal into it.

I didn't know what it was, but I had a bad feeling about it and I didn't want to keep it.

Turning away, I headed back down the path for the farm.

NINE

"WHERE HAVE YOU been?" Ivy demanded as soon I stepped through the door. "The day is half gone, and we've been slaving over quota while you run around getting...is that a *dress?*"

I took quick stock of the room—Ivy had risen from her chair by the fire. Gabe was still in his nest of blankets, his shoulder and back swathed in bandages, but he was sitting up and I noticed he had a pile of half-twisted yarn in his lap. He wasn't looking at me, but I could tell by the way he'd tensed his shoulders that he was very aware that I'd entered the room.

"Where's Jonn?" I asked. His chair was empty.

"He isn't feeling well, so he went to lie down." Ivy made a beeline to my side and tugged the dress from my arms. She held it up to the light. "Where did you get this? It's beautiful."

She said the word *beautiful* like an accusation.

I brushed past her for the kitchen. "From Ann."

Ivy ran her fingers over the lace, her mouth forming words that she didn't speak. It was rare that any of us touched such fine things.

I pulled the now-withered snow blossoms from my hair and let them drop to the floor before lifting the jug of milk from the windowsill where it kept cold and taking a long drink. Milk always made me feel fortified—our mother had always chuckled at my tendency to take a swig or two in preparation for something difficult. It wasn't exactly brandy, but it was what I did.

Ivy's sharp gaze didn't miss my actions. She followed me into the kitchen. "You went to see the Mayor, didn't you?"

I went past her into the main room again, heading straight for Gabe. I stopped in front of him and folded my arms. The Mayor's words echoed through my head. *Dangerous. Criminal.*

It was time the Farther and I had a chat.

"You're telling me everything. Now."

He took his time responding, like he was deliberately trying to make a point by making me wait. I tapped my foot. Finally he raised his head, and those ice-blue eyes sent a shiver down my spine.

"Why should I tell you anything?"

His words were belligerent, but he was stalling, bluffing. His hands trembled a little as he adjusted the blanket over himself.

I crouched down so that we were nose to nose. "Because I dragged you out of the Watcher-infested woods, cleaned your wounds, and nursed your fever. Because I'm currently lying to the Mayor of our village about your existence, at least by omission, not to mention by harboring you I'm putting my own family in jeopardy. And because I think I deserve to know. Should I keep going?"

"You lied to the Mayor?" Ivy squeaked from behind me.

I waved a hand at her to be quiet.

Gabe swallowed hard. "In my country, people could be killed for knowing the wrong things," he whispered.

"Here, not knowing is more likely to get you killed," I said. "So tell me."

He nodded slowly.

"Let's start with what the Mayor said." I sat down in the chair across from him and folded my arms. "He said you were dangerous. He said you were a criminal."

Gabe was still. His gaze shifted from mine to the wall above my head, like he was steeling himself for an unpleasant topic. "And did you believe him?"

"I don't know. *Are* you a criminal?"

His chest rose and fell as he took a breath. He stared at his fingers, and his jaw flexed as he considered his words. "I'm sure that's what they are calling me."

"*They?*"

"The soldiers looking for me."

I inhaled. I'd seen all the signs—he was wounded, he was frightened, he'd accused me of wanting to turn him in. But here it was, laid out starkly for me. "You're a fugitive, then."

"Yes," he said simply.

I waited for him to offer more. He flexed his fingers, not meeting my eyes. "What do you know about my country, Aeralis?"

"It is south of here," I said, searching my memory for every detail I knew. "You have inventions that we do not—airships, lamps lit by gas, instruments that play music without anyone touching them."

"What else?" he pressed. "What do you know of our political situation?"

I hesitated. I'd heard more, but I felt awkward bringing up the horror stories. How did I tell him that we considered his people cruel and sadistic? I tried to speak the words without inflection. "I—I've seen the soldiers pass by on the border roads with convoys of prisoners."

He lowered his head. "I was on one of those convoys. I was a prisoner."

Silence descended over us like a spell. I remembered the people I'd seen on the roads that

90

skirted the Frost. In my mind's eye I saw their faces, haggard and gaunt. Their hollow gazes. Suddenly I wanted to jump up and clap my fingers over Ivy's ears so she wouldn't hear the grim story I knew he was about to tell us. But I couldn't move.

"I lived in our capital city, Astralux. There has been much unrest there—our new leader, Merris, took power without bloodshed, but he has been keeping it through violence and suppression. My family..." he hesitated, choosing his words carefully. "We did not support his rise to power. His spies watched us, followed us, threatened us. And then one night they took me."

He paused, staring into space as if reliving the experience in his mind. "I was at a party and they came. They surrounded me, dragged me out. I was not allowed to say goodbye. I had no trial. Nothing. I was imprisoned." He paused, glancing at Ivy. In a lowered voice, he said, "They cut off the ends of my cell mate's fingers. I thought...I *feared* what they might do to me, too."

My mouth went dry as I remembered his delirious pleadings when he'd been sick, and how he'd screamed and entreated his invisible tormentors not to kill his family. Shudders crawled across my skin.

"I was prepared to tell them anything they wanted to know, but they didn't ask any questions." He looked disgusted with himself. "I didn't want to be tortured. I was a coward."

"No," I said, because I didn't know what else to say. Would I behave differently in the same situation?

Gabe shook his head, but he didn't argue with me. He continued the story. "After days of waiting, pleading, the jailers came. Stupidly, I thought I was delivered. But then they put me on the back of a wagon with others— other prisoners—and took us away."

91

"Where?" Ivy burst out.

I wanted to tell her to go outside, but I didn't speak. I couldn't bring myself to interrupt him.

"I heard one of the soldiers say they were taking us west."

Her eyes widened.

West. Chills rippled over my skin. I'd heard rumors about places where the prisoners were as thin as skeletons and the never-ending smoke smudged the horizon. It was far from our village, at the place where the snow began to thaw. There was nothing but mud and sickness.

Gabe took a deep breath. "We made camp along the road during the night. They chained us up like dogs because the other prisoners were resisting...they were afraid of being eaten by monsters from the forest. We'd all heard the stories, although the soldiers said the creatures wouldn't come as far as the roads."

I nodded. The Watchers never left the Frost.

Gabe continued, "One of the soldiers detached from the rest and wandered over to smoke at the edge of the forest, close to where I was chained. She pretended to drop her smokes and then she drew this shape in the ground." He picked up a stick from the edge of the fireplace and dragged the burned end across the stones, one long line and then a short one branching off it, like a warped Y. "She whispered that she was part of a group called the Thorns and that she was going to help me escape."

He leaned forward and smudged out the mark with his fingers before flinging the stick into the fire. "She unlocked my chains and told me to flee as soon as everyone was distracted. Then she went back to the others and began arguing with one of them. They started a fist fight, and I slipped into the darkness."

Ivy and I leaned forward, hanging on every word. "I was supposed to meet my contact outside your village, in the forest, but I never got that far. The soldiers realized I'd escaped and pursued me. I was shot, but it began to snow and they lost me in the blizzard. Night was falling, and they were afraid of the monsters, so they fell back. I heard them saying that I would be eaten, that they wouldn't bother pursuing across the river. I managed to drag myself as far as where you found me before I collapsed."

I shuddered to remember how close we'd come to leaving him there. "What about this gate Ivy said you mentioned?" I asked. "What is that?"

His expression shifted into something hopeful. "You've heard of it?"

"No."

"The Thorn agent said it was the only place I'll truly be safe from them, that it was imperative that I reach it. She said the Thorn contact here in the Frost would take me."

I'd never heard so much as a mention of this gate in my life, but if it was a Thorn place then I supposed that made sense. "Is that all you know?"

His forehead wrinkled as he thought. "She said only that it was an ancient thing, part of a ruin found deep in the Frost. She called it Echlos."

My mind buzzed. I thought of the map I'd seen on the Mayor's desk. I'd gotten only a glimpse, but it had been enough. Every inch of my skin prickled.

Echlos.

"What is it?" Gabe asked, seeing my expression.

I shook my head. I had to puzzle this out first. I had to think.

93

Could there really be such a thing, this gate, located at that place I'd seen inscribed on the map? Did the Mayor know of it? Did that mean he knew of the Thorns?

Gabe sighed and looked at the fire. "Is there anyone in the village that you believe might be working with the Thorns?"

"No," I said. I couldn't imagine any of our neighbors secretly smuggling runaways north. The people of the village cared for their own safety.

But I was beginning to wonder if that was really true—and more, if it should be true. How could we bury our heads in the snow and ignore the injustice that was happening around us?

Gabe nodded at my words. He couldn't quite keep the disappointment off his face "I see."

"What do you plan to do once you're healed?" I asked.

"I have to try to find this gate the Thorns told me about," he said. "It's my way out, my escape." He looked at me. "Can you help me?"

I bit my lip. "I don't know yet." It was the most honest thing I could tell him. "I'll have to think about it."

I had so many things to think about. His story, whether or not I believed him, and what I would do about it if I did.

TEN

IVY AND I were in the kitchen, making supper. The grim details of his story still clung to my memory, though I did my best to think of anything and everything else.

"Why is he working on the quota?" I asked, remembering the yarn in his lap.

"Jonn had to lie down because he wasn't feeling well, and I was falling behind," Ivy explained. "He's not too bad, either, for someone who's never done a bit of work in their life."

"Why do you say that?" I frowned at her.

Ivy glanced over her shoulder and then lowered her voice. "Have you seen his hands? They're as smooth as a baby's cheek. He's never done a second of farm labor before, I'd bet a week's quota on it."

"He said he lived in Aeralis' capital city, Astralux." The words felt strange on my tongue. *Astralux. City.* I'd never been to such a place, although I'd heard about cities in school. I knew they were like villages, only much bigger and much more crowded. I'd even seen photographs that belonged to a merchant from the south, but they had been dark and smudged.

"Perhaps his father was a sort of mayor?" Ivy suggested.

I peeked around the corner at him. Come to think of it, he did have a noble bearing, the kind that all the Elder families had. That kind of dignity had to be bred into a person. "Maybe," I said. But I was distracted by the way

95

his hair fell into his eyes, and the way the firelight played across his nose and mouth and made shadows on them.

Gabe sensed me watching and looked up. Our eyes met. I turned and went back into the kitchen, where I rattled the plates and banged the pots to settle my jumping stomach.

"What are we going to do about him?" Ivy asked, still whispering.

"I don't know," I said, irritable. Everyone was expecting me to have it all figured out, but I didn't.

I filled the kettle and took it out to the main room to put over the fire. We had a stove, of course, but it was fickle and we could barely use the top for anything. The fireplace was better. It had an iron spit, and I hung the kettle on it. I could feel Gabe's eyes on my back as I stoked the flames.

"You were going to tell your Mayor about me today, weren't you?" he asked.

I was silent. I poked at the coals with the fire iron.

"What made you change your mind?"

I thought about hearing my parents' names, about the crawling feeling between my shoulder blades when the Mayor smiled at me, how Gabe screamed when he'd been sick. I thought about how the Mayor described Gabe as dangerous even though he'd been weak and helpless in the barn, and how he'd been kind to my sister and how he'd thanked me when I saved his life. All these things ran through my head in a waterfall of images and feelings, and I didn't have any words to describe them.

"It didn't feel right," I said, but as soon as I spoke the words they seemed ridiculous. *It didn't feel right?* What was right, though? *Right* was telling the Mayor and leaving it in his hands. *Right* was avoiding contact with the Farthers.

96

Wasn't it?

Feeling unsettled, I got up and went to check on Jonn.

He was lying asleep on the bed that had previously belonged to our parents. I put a quilt over him so he'd stay warm before returning to the fire.

"How's your brother?" Gabe asked. His eyebrows drew together as he peered at me.

"He's fine." I picked up the yarn that he'd finished twisting and began rolling it into a ball, my fingers working automatically. "He's just sleeping."

"He's sick, isn't he? What happened to him?"

I looked up. Gabe's expression was free of pity, disgust, or condemnation, all things I was used to seeing in the villagers' eyes. He looked merely curious.

"The farm is dangerous. Equipment fails, things fall, people make mistakes." I hesitated, sifting through the words in my head, choosing them carefully. "There was an accident involving an overturned wagon. Jonn's leg was crushed, along with part of his midsection and some of his skull. It is a miracle that his intestines didn't rupture, they say. He was five years old."

I checked his reaction. Gabe was silent, listening.

Drawing in a breath, I continued, "The leg never healed right, and his health never recovered. He is prone to seizures sometimes, and he does not walk without assistance. Now he is essentially an invalid, living here with me instead of starting his own family with their own quota. He's old enough to marry, but who would want to marry a cripple?"

There was more to the story, but I didn't tell him all the details, like how my parents had to fight for the doctor to operate on Jonn to save his life. How they had to work extra hard to keep up with the work load since

97

he was too weak to help but our expected output hadn't changed. How we'd all picked up the slack Jonn left.

Gabe gazed at the fire a moment without speaking. "And you had no doctors to repair the leg, no medicine to heal his seizures?" he asked finally.

"Just the village physician, and his knowledge is limited. There was nothing else that could be done. We're lucky he survived at all."

We worked silently a few moments while Gabe considered this. And it was strange, I thought, because it felt almost good to tell our sad story to this strange Farther boy who'd never heard it. It was like I'd been holding my breath for years, and now I was finally allowed to let it out.

"In Aeralis, the doctors could have fixed him," he said.

"I know." My hands slowed as I looked at him. "But didn't you know that the people of the Frost have nothing to do with the Farthers?"

We shared a sad smile at the irony of my words.

"I don't understand why, though," he said after another moment.

"Why what?"

"Watchers, snowstorms, hard life on the farm... Why do you live here in the Frost if life is so dangerous?"

I laughed. "Where else are we supposed to live? It's our home. We've been living here as long as anyone can remember."

Gabe shook his head stubbornly. "What I mean was, why settle here in the first place?"

It was a fair question, so I considered it. "There is a bird here in the Frost called the bluewing. It's a tiny bird, small enough to sit in the palm of my hand. Nearly every hawk and eagle preys upon it. But this bird does a funny thing. It makes its home in a poisonous thorny bush

98

called stingweed, where one prick from the thorns would knock it dead."

"Dead? Then why...?"

"Why does it live in a place that could kill it?" I shrugged. "None of the predatory birds will attack it there, because they are too large—they'd be poisoned by the branches for sure, where the smaller bird is just the right size to slip in and out safely, and it has learned the tricks. It's a perilous dance of survival for the bluewing, flying in and out of that bush every day without getting stung, but the bird is just small enough and just nimble enough to navigate most of the time. And in the bush, he is protected from his greatest threat."

Gabe hesitated. "And what does the Frost protect your people from?" he asked.

I didn't mince my words. "Farthers."

He nodded, looking at his hands. "I guess my people have always been a threat to yours, haven't they?"

"My parents used to say that our place here has kept us from being absorbed and enslaved by your Empire. We once valued our freedom enough to risk everything for it, but perhaps, if I'm being honest, we just don't know anything else but this place anymore. Life isn't perfect here, Gabe. It's a perilous dance every day just like with the bluewing, and sometimes I wonder if it's worth it. Our every action is wrapped up in preserving our safety. We're so sheltered here. What kind of a life is that?"

Gabe didn't say anything.

I laughed under my breath, and it sounded bitter. "Listen to me. What am I talking about, *worth it?* Is any experience or bit of beauty worth the cost of my life? I know nothing but safety and self-preservation at all costs."

99

"And yet," he said softly, "you're risking everything to help me."

I nodded, looking at the fire. Silence wrapped around us like a blanket, and it was surprisingly soothing to sit without speaking in his presence.

"What about you?" he asked after a long pause. "Do you have any plans for the future?"

"Me?"

"You said earlier that your brother couldn't marry. Do you plan to marry?"

I could hear Ivy still banging pots in the kitchen. I wanted to brush off his question, but I'd done so much talking already that the words poured out of me like water, good idea or not. "Well, it's expected of me. A family is the best way to strengthen the village and make it safe, and that is our greatest value."

"Strength?"

"Safety," I said. And in that moment I realized that I'd always equated the two in my head, but they weren't the same thing. Sometimes people were strongest at their most vulnerable, dangerous moments.

Gabe interrupted my musings with another question. "You don't want to marry?"

"It's not that, exactly." How could I explain? "We are orphans. My parents died a few months ago in an accident much like Jonn's, and I am now the head of the household. If I marry, I will be expected to leave them and move in with my new husband. None of the men in this village would want to provide for my siblings, too. I don't know what will become of them. Ivy will probably be taken in by a more established family until she is grown, and Jonn..."

I didn't know what would happen to my twin. His best qualities, quiet calmness and level-headedness and a sense of humor despite all obstacles, were not high in

100

demand when it came to quota-meeting. He could not walk or run, and that made him lesser somehow in the eyes of the villagers.

"I worry," I whispered, "that I won't be able to look after them anymore."

Gabe nodded, and the moment was suddenly too personal, too intimate. Our eyes met. My chest felt hollow and full at the same time, and I recognized it for what it was—desire. I found him attractive. Flustered, I picked up my work and went to the loom.

"What is that?" Gabe asked, looking at the loom. Thankfully, it didn't seem as though he'd sensed my discomfort.

"You're joking."

"I'm not."

I ran my fingers over the loom. "A loom. It spins the wool into thread," I said. "But Ivy and I are the only ones who can use it, obviously, and I'm much better at it than Ivy. The yarn we twist by hand, and we have to deliver both to make quota." I considered his question again. "Do you *really* mean to say that you've never seen a loom before?"

Gabe shrugged. "I really haven't."

I found this incredible. "How do the Farthers make clothing, then?"

He laughed. "I don't have the slightest idea. Factories, I suppose."

"Factories?"

"You know. Where they make things. Each person does a tiny part, and it goes much faster."

I sat down on the hearth. "And different families run these things, these factories?"

He shook his head. "No. People from hundreds of different families work there. It's a business. They get paid money. There isn't a family quota, not like here."

I knew what money was, of course. Merchants that came through in the spring carried it, and children liked to find dropped pieces on the road and play with them. We'd even learned about it in school, but we didn't use it here. "No quota? Not even your family?"

"Certainly not my family," Gabe said, blushing slightly.

I blinked. Even the Mayor's family had to meet quota, however small and frivolous their contribution might be. "Everyone contributes here in our village. What did you family do all day? Work in a factory?"

He cleared his throat. "My, ah, my father was a wealthy man. We had servants, money... The people in my family spent most of their time at parties and balls. Or riding—we had horses. Land."

Had. I wondered what the state of his family's things was now.

"Are they safe?" I asked, softly. I didn't know how to ask delicately if they were in as much trouble as he was.

"I don't know." I could see the pain that flickered in his eyes. "No one told me anything about them. The last time I saw them was the night I was seized." He paused, considering his words. "I was taken by the soldiers in front of my sister. I remember when they dragged me out. She was crying, but she wasn't making any noise. There she stood in her ball gown. It was her birthday. One of the soldiers hit me across the face with the butt of his rifle—he smashed my nose in—and some of the blood got on the fabric when she tried to help me."

He broke off and swallowed hard. "The whole thing was like a dream. I was so certain I was going to wake up, but...life is a nightmare now."

Taken by soldiers from his sister's birthday party? Beaten in the face? I touched his arm gently, wanting only to comfort him. He turned his head, meeting my

102

eyes, and then together we looked at my hand against his arm. I withdrew it, embarrassed, but he reached out and caught my fingers.

"Thank you," he said. "For staying with me while I was sick. I don't remember much from that night, but I remember you were there. You treated me with kindness."

I wanted to say that it was nothing, but that wasn't true and we both knew it. The air grew thick around us, and my heart throbbed with the kind of sweet pain that comes with wanting something you aren't sure you can even dare to ask for.

In that moment, we were not a Farther and a Frost girl. We were just two people, and I was astonished at how easy it was to forget that there were any other barriers between us.

ELEVEN

THE DAYS PASSED slowly. We worked at quota while the snow fell outside, because there was nothing else to do in the winter months but work at inside projects and hope the Watchers stayed away. I continued to see tracks across the path into the village and around the perimeter of our yard, but no more claw marks breached the unbroken field of white between the house and the barn, for which I was grateful. The snow piled up in drifts, and Ivy and I struggled to clear a path before the farmhouse door and the barn. Snowshoes became necessary for trekking across the fields and around the edges of the farm.

Gabe grew stronger every day. Soon his injury began to heal into an ugly pink scar, and he stopped screaming in his dreams as his fevers ceased completely.

Another week, another quota due, and I took the sack of thread and yarn into town. I avoided Cole because I didn't know how to dissuade his interest in me and I didn't have the energy to argue with him about it. I tried to speak to Ann, but every time I went into town she was either missing or surrounded by friends. I wasn't able to get her away from the others, but it probably didn't matter anyway. Even if I had managed to have a private conversation with her, I didn't know what I would say.

In every Assembly I attended, I stared hard at the back of every head in front of me, trying to imagine who could be working with the Thorns. Such outside contact—with Farthers, no less—was strictly forbidden. Who would have dared to risk it, and why?

One day I returned home to find Gabe showing Jonn how to walk with the help of what he called *dual crutches*, which worked far better than Jonn's pitiful single crutch that he occasionally used to hobble around. Jonn demonstrated his new freedom by traveling to the kitchen and back, and when he finally plunked down in his chair by the fire we all burst into enthusiastic applause at his efforts.

Gabe caught me smiling and said I looked very nice when I smiled, and that made me disinclined to smile, and I told him so. He replied I was a difficult girl to understand, and I told him that maybe if he weren't such a simpleton he wouldn't think so, because everyone else in the village seemed to make perfect sense of me. Ivy broke in to our bickering and said that our flirting was making everyone else uncomfortable, and that shut us both up, although I swear I saw Gabe smile before he turned his head. And even though I was partly angry at him, I *wanted* to smile, too.

It was madness.

I was no closer to deciding what to do about Gabe, either. ("You've stopped calling him 'Farther,'" Ivy noted aloud one afternoon.) I knew he couldn't stay here in the Frost, although thinking it made me restless and unhappy. Twice again I went into the village with the intent to tell the Mayor, and twice more I lost my nerve. Once I even ran into Adam Brewer in the streets, and he opened his mouth to say something to me, but I put my head down and passed on quickly before he could.

At the house, Gabe was growing increasingly restless as he began to heal. He kept asking me questions about the mysterious gate, questions I couldn't answer. I forbid Ivy to ask them in the village. But my mind kept returning to the map I'd seen in the Mayor's study. If only I'd gotten a better glimpse.

By the three week mark, Gabe had grown well enough to move cautiously around the house and yard. Having him around had increased our quota, which thankfully had afforded us extra supplies with which to feed him. Now he was helping with the barn chores, too. Of course, I was in no way becoming accustomed to or even happy about his presence. Absolutely not, because that would mean that I liked him.

But for some reason I kept finding excuses to stay around the house.

"Did you find anything out about the Thorns contact?" Gabe asked me one day as I closed the door behind me. I'd just returned from the weekly Assembly. He was stretched on his pallet by the fireplace, reading a book that must have belonged to my parents. I'd never had much use for books—never had enough time.

"No." I crossed the room with a sigh, glancing around. "Where are my brother and sister?"

"Jonn said he'd see to the horses tonight, and Ivy wandered off." He put the book face-down on his chest and folded his hands over it. "Have you been asking around the town about them?"

I went to the window and peered out. I hadn't seen either of them when I'd returned. Worry pinched my stomach, but I brushed it away. I worried a lot, and it never helped anything. There was still daylight yet. "What am I supposed to do? March into the square and ask if anyone is working with them? I have to be cautious."

He frowned. "Pretty soon I'll be healed, and then what will we do? I can't hide here forever. You can't keep feeding me forever, either."

106

I turned away from the window, restless. The conversation was making me irritable, and I didn't know why. "What are you reading?"

He looked down at the book. "I found it upstairs in the attic. It's called *The Winter Parables*. Mostly love poems so far." His expression turned devilish. "Maybe you could read a few to Cole Carver."

My cheeks flushed. What lies had Ivy told him? "Poems are stupid, sappy things. I don't even know why my parents have that book."

Gabe's eyes followed me as I crossed the room to the kitchen. I think he was suppressing a smile behind that little smirk of his. I wanted nothing more than to wipe it off his face.

"Why are you reading love poetry, anyway? Thinking about Lakin?"

As soon as I'd said the name I regretted it. Gabe's eyes darkened. I put a hand over my mouth and leaned against the wall. "I—I'm sorry—"

"Where did you hear that name?" His tone was tense, quiet.

My heart thudded. "You said it in your delirium. You thought she was me."

"Did I say anything more?"

"Not really." A horrified blush covered my cheeks. Why had I brought this up?

He waited.

I relented. "You mentioned something about a promise. You said you were sorry. But you didn't say much more than that. Not that I could understand, anyway."

Gabe frowned and looked down, and I felt ten kinds of horrible for bringing it up at all. Was this Lakin someone who had betrayed him?

107

After a moment, he lifted his head and saw my consternation.

"Hey," he said softly. "I'm sorry. I don't mean to make you feel like you've done something wrong."

"Who was she?" I whispered.

"Lakin is—*was*—my betrothed."

"Oh. Your betrothed."

Why did I feel so sick to my stomach? And then I realized he'd said *was*. I felt even sicker. "Is she—I mean has she...?"

"No, no," he said. "She's fine. We broke off the engagement months ago, although we remained friends. Her connection to me when I was arrested was tenuous at best, so I am sure she is safe from being associated with my new criminal status."

We smiled awkwardly—it wasn't funny, but when everything was a disaster you had to find humor somewhere. Silence fell between us.

"So you were betrothed," I said aloud, testing the word out. "You seem young for it."

I didn't really know if he was too young to be married or not—I knew little about the marriage customs of his people, and I didn't know his exact age either. I was mostly just fishing for information, quite shamelessly so.

He rubbed his forehead, looking abashed. "It was arranged when we were barely older than children, you see, but neither of us minded the arrangement. We were friends."

"Why'd you break it off?"

As soon as I'd asked, I felt breathless. Was I being too forward?

He ran one finger up and down the spine of the book on his chest. "There was trouble between our families. It had nothing to do with us, really, but we couldn't marry after everything settled."

"Were you sorry?" I spoke the words so quietly that I didn't know if he'd heard them.

He had heard. His eyes searched mine. "Yes and no. I cared for her, but it was not passionate glances and stolen kisses, you see. I think we each would have wanted more than the other could give, in the end."

When he said *stolen kisses*, I felt hot and cold. I wanted to look away, but I couldn't.

The door behind me burst open and Ivy rushed in, her arms full of fresh snow blossoms. Gabe and I moved apart.

"I saw that we were running out of dried ones..." She scanned our faces and broke off, smiling slyly. "Am I interrupting anything?"

"Let me have those," I said. "Where's Jonn?"

She handed me the snow blossoms, still grinning. "He's coming."

I avoided Gabe's eyes after she went back outside. The mood had shattered, leaving awkwardness in its wake. I went to hang the blossoms from the drying rack in the kitchen.

"Lia?" Gabe asked.

I turned.

"What I said about Lakin and kisses. I wasn't...I mean I'm not..." He blushed again. "That was very direct. I'm not trying to be improper."

"I need to make supper," I said, and went into the kitchen.

Leaning against the sink, I covered my eyes with my hand. What was wrong with me? I moved away from Cole's advances, but when Gabe mentioned kisses I melted inside.

109

Sometimes I didn't understand myself in the slightest.

~

We were struck with unseasonable warmth for a day, and the sun warmed the snow until it softened. The freeze the next night turned the snow into a crunchy shell that encapsulated the landscape in a sleek white crust. The whole world looked encased in glass.

It was a quiet day on the farm. Ivy was visiting a friend in town, and Jonn was playing his flute indoors, the sound of it like birdsong. Gabe had volunteered to help with the barn chores, insisting that he was healed enough to pitch in with the rest of us.

I lingered by the door, plucking a handful of fresh snow blossoms for my pocket when I heard a shout.

Gabe.

I scrambled across the snow, my snowshoes hissing as they skidded and slid over the icy crust. I spotted him by the paddock, no Watchers or villagers in sight. My heartbeat slowed, and I almost laughed at the panic that had gripped me.

"Gabe?"

The wind blew his hair across his face, so I didn't see his dismayed expression until I got close.

"What...?" I looked past him and saw. The fence, which had been in a state of disrepair since my father died, had toppled over. The horses had escaped.

I spun in a circle, my eyes scanning the yard. One grazed on tufts of grass that stuck out above the snow beside the barn wall.

The other was missing.

And his tracks led straight into the forest.

I wasted no time catching the first horse. His lead rope dangled off his halter, and I crept up beside him and snagged it. He just looked at me with his big brown eyes and shook his mane. I led him inside and put him in his stall before returning to join Gabe, who had hobbled to the fence and crouched down to examine it.

I knew what must be done. I strode to his side and faced the woods.

My hands felt stiff and tingly as I stared at the shifting shadows and evergreen branches. I hadn't been in the forest since we'd found Gabe. Memories of the encroaching darkness, the slick swath of blood on the snow flashed through my mind in little lightning bursts. Just the thought of returning made my stomach sick.

"What are you going to do?" Gabe stood and brushed the snow from his hands. He looked at me with a worried frown. I think he already knew my answer, and he looked unhappy about it. We'd never said much about the Watchers, but he was aware of their existence.

"Well," I said, exhaling a cloud of breath. "I can't lose the horse. It doesn't belong to us. We just board it here during the winter." I chewed my lip as reality of exactly what I was about to do sunk its cold claws into my chest. "I'll have to go after it."

"I'm going with you," he said, immediately.

"No."

His mouth turned down in a frown. "It wasn't a request, Lia."

"You aren't fully healed. You're still weak. If you can't keep up, then I have two problems to worry about."

"I'll keep up." His jaw clenched. "I'm a lot stronger than before."

"This is a bad idea," I said. The wind blew across my face, numbing my lips. I crossed my arms over my chest and glared at him.

111

"I'm not letting you go in there alone." Determination simmered in his eyes, and I was touched on a deep level in spite of my misgivings. But at the same time, what if he got hurt? He was still weak. I didn't like it.

"Lia, please."

It was late afternoon, and the sun had already begun to sink behind the trees. There was little time to argue, so I just started for the tree line without responding.

I heard the crunch of his footsteps as he followed after me, and anger simmered in my chest at his stubbornness. "Gabe—"

"Listen," he said. "If I get too tired, I'll turn around and go back. Fair enough?"

I didn't like it, but there wasn't time to protest.

"Fine." I stopped just before the foliage started. Taking a breath, I fumbled in my pocket for the blue ribbons I kept there. I drew one out and tied a snow blossom around a bare limb that stretched toward us like a bony finger.

"What's that for?" Gabe watched my actions with interest.

"It's what we're supposed to do when we go into the forest. It will help us if we get lost, and hopefully it'll form a wall of safety if any Watchers are roaming nearby."

"What is it with Watchers and snow blossoms?"

I finished tying the ribbon and left the blossom dangling. "I don't know. But the sight of them makes the monsters stop."

We stepped together into the forest, and despite all my protestations I was glad for the company. Bare trees formed a line of black bark against the crisp white of the snow. The world was alien and silent except for the rasp

112

of our snowshoes across the wintery surface. The horse's tracks formed a staggering line where he'd scrambled through the drifts.

"Stupid animal," I growled.

The light became bluer and darker as we moved deeper into the forest. I kept tying ribbons and blossoms on the trees. I lost track of how long we'd been gone—the forest had that effect—but I kept tying blossoms on the branches and I kept moving.

"You're doing a better job of keeping up than I thought you would," I admitted to Gabe after a while.

We rounded a cluster of naked trees and entered a clearing. A frozen pond lay like glass in the middle, reflecting the sunlight, and the horse's path led right into it. The ice in the center had shattered, and a path of dark water led straight to the other side. We skirted the edges slowly.

His breath made a cloud in front of his mouth. "I'm healing." He swung his arm to demonstrate, wincing a little as he did so.

I was silent as the realization settled over me. Healing meant soon there would be no more reason for him to stay. This should have made me happy, because it would mean our safety. But it didn't.

We reached the end of the pond, where the horse had exited the water. The tracks led up a hill and out of sight. I stood looking up. "What will you do when you're strong enough to go?"

He shuffled his feet to warm them. His eyes slid away from mine, toward the tracks. "I can't go back. I can't stay here."

We both knew the truth. Gabe was the one to say it.

"I need to get to that place the Thorns operative told me about."

113

"Here's the problem," I said, starting up the snow-crusted rock. "I've never heard of it in my life. I have no idea where it is, and these forests are dangerous. We could spend months looking for it and never come close to finding it. And with the Watchers, we can't spend too much time wandering around. We'd have to know exactly where to go."

We reached the top of the hill. My eyes swept the clearing, and my breath left me in a punch of shock.

A man stood with his back to us.

I could see only his thick homespun cloak and his dark hair. A villager. Our feet crunched loudly against the snow, announcing our presence, and two thoughts went through my mind—Gabe was with me and this man would ask who he was.

The figure began to turn, and I knew we were caught against the white snow with nowhere to hide without being seen. I grabbed Gabe's shirt with both hands and pulled him forward. I caught one glimpse of his widened eyes before I did the one thing I could think of to do, the one thing that would explain who he was and why he was with me and why we were about to flee upon being discovered.

I kissed him.

His lips were cold and rough. He froze for a split second before cupping my face with both hands, kissing me back. Then, as if noticing the villager for the first time, I pushed Gabe behind the bushes, against the trunk of a tree, and broke away.

"Lia," Gabe whispered. His eyes were dark and startled as they met mine, and his fingers gripped my shoulder, keeping me from pulling away.

"There was someone," I responded, and he went still as he understood me. I held up one finger and backed away, stepping back into the clearing.

114

He was still there, and my heart sunk like a stone as I recognized him.

Adam Brewer.

The wind teased my hair, and my lips stung where they'd been pressed against Gabe's. Adam faced me. Here we stood, both in the forest in the dying light of late afternoon. The lengthening shadows suddenly seemed oppressive, and every tree seemed to hide an enemy. I shivered.

"Lia Weaver," he said quietly, acknowledging me with a curt nod of his head. His dark hair brushed his eyebrows. "Yarn doesn't grow on trees in this forest."

What was he trying to imply?

I lifted my chin. I couldn't avoid answering him now, no matter what I thought of him. I'd been cornered. "Adam Brewer. I don't see you carrying a keg." The words came out too haughty, too sharp. I was supposed to be making nice so he wouldn't ask questions, but I couldn't help myself.

His eyebrows knit together as he frowned. "I am chopping firewood," he said.

My gaze dropped to his empty hands. Silence hung between us as we sized each other up, guessing each other's secrets.

"I am looking for my horse," I said finally. "He ran off. Have you seen him?"

Adam shook his head. His dark eyes narrowed slightly, but when he spoke his tone was polite. "Do you need assistance?"

"No, I..." My voice trailed off. I gestured at the trees behind me.

"You and a beau are seeing to it," he finished for me. "I saw you a moment ago."

115

I didn't say anything. My heart thumped hard in my chest. Would he leave us alone? Would he ask questions? Would he tell somebody?

Adam tipped his head to one side. "I wouldn't have pegged you for a risk-taker, Lia Weaver."

A blush touched my cheeks and evaporated against the cold. "I'm full of surprises."

"Indeed. Perhaps you might want to choose a safer place for your romantic trysts. These forests are full of Watchers. Perhaps your parents' barn would be better, above the place where the stones form a circle."

A chill rippled over me. The words were strange, nosy. I didn't answer him. He turned to leave, pausing to study my face one more time.

Why did I feel as if he could see straight to my soul?

A sigh escaped me when he vanished from sight. Behind me, Gabe emerged from the bushes with a rustle of branches.

"That was close." He sounded as breathless as I felt. "Did he see me?"

"Yes, and yes. But I don't think he got a good look. He...assumed things about you, and left it at that. He knew I'd be reluctant to give way to prying."

I didn't elaborate further. I was *not* discussing the kiss.

"You seemed like you knew each other," Gabe observed. Was that a note of jealousy in his tone?

I ran my fingers up and down the edge of my cloak. Even just talking about it made my skin itch. "His parents were with mine when they died. They'd asked my father to do them a favor, and something went wrong."

"Wrong?"

"Watchers," I said softly. The word burned on my tongue, and for a moment there was nothing but the

116

sound of the wind. Snow began to drift down from the sky like feathers, landing on my lashes and catching in his hair. I didn't tell him the rest—how the Brewers had denied being with my parents at all, how they'd claimed we were making up lies about them, how they swore they hadn't been in the forest when my parents had been killed, even though I'd seen one of them leave with my mother and father—I'd seen them step together into the woods with my own eyes through the window in my bedroom. They'd lured my parents to their deaths and then denied the whole thing. And then they'd thrown me and my siblings to the wolves in the process.

"Oh." Gabe looked like he wanted to say something else, but as far as I was concerned the conversation was finished. I stamped off after the horse tracks, and he followed.

We found the horse beyond the next grove of trees, grazing on a patch of ice-coated grass. I slipped alongside him and grabbed his halter. The horse snorted at me, and I scowled.

"You've caused a lot of trouble," I snapped at him. "Come on, now." I tugged on the lead rope, leading the horse to a fallen tree trunk where I took my snowshoes off and hung them around my neck. Hoisting myself up onto the horse's broad back, which was wet from dripping snow, I grabbed his mane and wrapped both legs around his shaggy sides. "Hurry. We should hurry back." The light was already beginning to fade.

Gabe stepped to the side of the horse and removed his snowshoes just like I'd done. He stepped onto the tree trunk and surveyed the horse's back with a determined expression.

I realized his shoulder was probably bothering him. I offered him my hand, and he accepted. A tingle ran up my arm at the way our palms fit together, but I brushed the thought away and tugged him up behind me. He kept a careful distance between us. Having him so close tied my stomach into knots. I cleared my throat nervously.

Laying the lead rope against the horse's neck and squeezing my legs against his sides, I urged him forward at a trot.

"How well do you know these woods?" Gabe asked from behind me. The horse stumbled as he descended the hill, and he grabbed my shoulders for balance.

"I used to travel them with my father," I said, breathless because of the sudden contact. He let go of me a moment later, and I felt almost disappointed about it. I kept talking, half to distract myself and half because I didn't know how to stop. "He was a trapper as well as a weaver. We put the extra meat in our cooking pot and traded the extra pelts in the market." Just talking about it made my throat squeeze tight. "He knew these forests as well as he knew his own name. He was fearless when it came to the Watchers, too. But then..."

I didn't really want to finish that thought, so I let it dangle. In my mind's eye I saw the men who had come to our door and the heavy blankness that had filled their eyes as they'd delivered the news. I saw Ivy, hunched over and sobbing, Jonn's face wiped of expression. I remembered the utter numbness that had gripped me, and the crushing realization that my family's fate was in my hands now.

Hesitantly, I began to tell Gabe about what I'd had to do to keep the family together. He listened without speaking as I poured out my fears, my worries. I'd never told anybody this before, but for some reason I found myself spilling every secret terror to him. Maybe it was because he'd accompanied me into the forest so willingly. Maybe it was because when he listened to me I felt heard in a way I'd never experienced before.

118

When I finished, it felt as if a huge weight had been lifted from my shoulders. I exhaled. Gabe was quiet. Then his hand touched my arm. Slowly, his arms slipped around me until he was holding me. I relaxed against him like my whole body was sighing into him, and warmth crept over my skin even though I was freezing cold.

"Lia—"

An inhuman shriek split the air, and all the hairs on my arm stood up. The horse danced sideways, tossing his head. Gabe jerked, swiveling to look behind us. "What was that?"

Realization skittered over my skin like shards of ice. The shadows had grown too long, the darkness too complete. It was almost night, and we were still in the forest.

I whispered the words.

"A Watcher."

TWELVE

I TURNED THE horse in a tight circle. My heart hammered and my breath came in harsh gasps as I tried to think. It would do us no good to flee straight into the creature's path. I scanned the gathering shadows, and then I saw it—a ripple of movement against the dark, a rustle of fur and feathers and a squeal that sounded like metal against metal.

The horse shied away and laid his ears back.

"Hold on," I gritted to Gabe, and then I dug my heels into the horse's sides.

The horse took off like a stone shot from a sling. The trees rushed past, branches slapping our faces and dragging at our bodies. I ducked low, burying myself in the mane of the horse. Gabe slid against me with every lurch of his stride. "Are we close to the edge of the forest?" he shouted into my ear.

I could see the yard. I urged the horse faster, and we flew into the clearing in a spray of snow. The shriek of the Watcher sounded again behind us, louder and closer. The horse thundered toward the barn. Gabe began to slip, and he wrapped both arms around my waist and hung on for dear life as we made a sharp turn around the side of the house.

We reached the door. I slid off and hit the ground running, my fingers wrenching at the door to get it open. Gabe flattened himself over the horse's back and kicked him forward. I threw down a handful of the snow blossoms onto the threshold and then rushed after them inside.

Ivy and Jonn recoiled as I slammed the door shut and threw the bolts into place. The Watcher howled outside, the sound far away and piercing.

We were safe.

The horse snorted and shook his mane. Gabe slid off his back and handed me the lead rope. He was breathing hard. Our eyes met, and we broke into desperate laughter. It was just too absurd—my siblings standing there with their mouths hanging open, the horse in the living room, and the Watcher unable to reach us and unwilling to cross the blossoms. And it wasn't even funny, but it was laugh or cry. So I laughed. Deep, belly-splitting laughs that bent me over. Gabe and I leaned together, howling with mirth while the others sat dumbfounded. Well, Jonn sat. Ivy stormed over to us and stood glaring.

"Lia Weaver, *what in the world*—"

"I found the horse," I interrupted, still giggling. "In the forest." Gabe leaned against the wall and laughed, his eyes squeezed shut. I liked the way he looked when he was happy, even if that happiness was pure delusion.

Ivy planted her hands on her hips, her mouth hanging open as she looked from me to Gabe to the horse. Apparently the whole situation—our laughter, the horse, our wild entrance—was simply too bizarre to merit any kind of comments, because she just acted like we didn't have a giant animal standing in the middle of our house. She zeroed in on me instead. "Since when did you get so jovial?" she asked, as if that were the most pressing question, like I'd committed some kind of crime.

121

The horse stamped one foot against the floorboards and snorted explosively as my grin weakened a little. Wasn't I allowed to laugh?

My gallows humor faded, and I straightened. Taking the poor horse's lead rope, I took him beside the window and tethered him to one of the coat hooks. I even gave him a pat on the neck—although I wasn't particularly fond of this animal, or any animals, I was glad he was safe and not eaten by a Watcher.

By the fire, Gabe began explaining what had happened while Ivy and Jonn listened intently. I stiffened when he reached the part about Adam Brewer, but he left out the kiss and simply described the scene as if I'd pushed him into the bushes and marched out to confront Adam on my own.

"How dare Adam Brewer ask *you* questions like that," Ivy growled, interrupting the story. "He—they—" Apparently there were no words to describe her feelings about the Brewers. I wholeheartedly agreed.

"Why they haven't been evicted from the village for their bad behavior, I don't know," she said.

"They always meet their quota," Jonn pointed out. That was my brother, generous with everyone.

"He said such cryptic things to me, too," I said slowly, remembering that moment in the woods and the way he'd been so cold, so rigid while the snow fell between us. "Like he was expecting something from me, something specific, and he was disappointed when I didn't deliver it."

"He probably wanted you to get angry. Maybe he was hoping you'd accuse him," Ivy said.

What was it he'd said at the end?

I wouldn't have pegged you for a risk-taker. That boiled my blood a little. It was like he was calling me

122

cowardly. And perhaps I would have agreed with him a month ago, but now...

I looked at Ivy and Jonn and Gabe—Gabe describing the part where we caught the horse, the others listening with rapt attention.

Some things were worth taking a risk for.

He'd said something else to me, something odd, but I couldn't quite remember what it was.

We spent the night by the fire, wrapped in quilts. The horse huffed and nickered quietly in the corner, and I listened to the sound of my family sleeping. I fell asleep in the middle of trying to figure out what exactly Adam Brewer had said to me before we'd parted, and while I slept I dreamed that I was lost in the forest again, only this time I was with Ann. We found our way home after hours of wandering, and she hugged me with relief, but when she put her arms around me she became Cole and then a creature with both fur and feathers, and red eyes that glowed in the dark. I knew it was a Watcher, and when I tried to run it ran at me with its jaws opened wide—

I woke abruptly. My skin was damp with sweat and my throat felt scratchy. I lay still a moment as my senses sharpened. Gradually, the room swam into focus.

Everyone else was still asleep, tangled up in the blankets and breathing deeply. Ivy was nestled against the hearth, her head pillowed in her hands. Gabe slept with his head in his arms and his elbows braced on his knees. Jonn was curled in his chair, the face that looked so much like mine soft and gentle in sleep.

Guilt stabbed me as I thought about how worried my brother must have been when we didn't return. Anything could have happened, and for all he knew, we'd simply gone to the barn.

Barn. That's what Adam Brewer had said to me—*perhaps you might want to choose a safer place for your romantic trysts...perhaps your parents' barn, above the place where the stones form a circle.*

The place where the stones for a circle? How oddly specific. How strange. What did he know of my parents' barn, and why had he spoken of it?

A suspicion curled in my gut.

I went to the window and threw back the shutters. It was early morning. A thread of orange light sparkled on the horizon and blazed across the top of the forest. The yard was silent. Nothing moved against the tree line.

The Watchers were gone.

Grabbing my cloak, I untied the horse and led him out into the chilly air. A soft light colored everything gray. Holding my breath, I led him across the yard to the barn.

Inside, the darkness swallowed us. I put the horse in his stall and fumbled along the wall for a lantern and the matches. The light flared; the horse nickered softly to his mate. My breath caught.

There, in the middle of the stone floor, was a pattern.

A circle.

I dropped to my knees, running my fingers across the stones, tracing the edges of the shape they made. I'd lived my whole life in this house and never really looked at the floor here—it was always covered in dust or straw. Always concealed.

Something touched my arm.

I whirled, gasping, and it was Gabe. He put a hand over my mouth and a finger to his lips. I nodded, my heart thumping. It might be morning, but there was no reason to take chances. The sun hadn't risen yet.

"You startled me," I whispered when he removed his hand.

"What are you doing?"

I gestured at the floor. "It was something Adam Brewer said. Remember? About the circle of stones in the barn. And there it is. How did he know?"

Gabe's forehead wrinkled. He crouched down beside the stones, staring. "What is it?"

"I have no idea."

I moved the lantern closer and knelt beside him on the ground. Sliding my hands along the edge, I felt them catch. I heard a click, and the circle moved. We scrambled back as a dark crack appeared in the stones. A piece of the floor slid aside, revealing a dark hole. A hollow place. Stairs.

"What the...?" I grabbed the lantern and peered into the darkness. My head spun with questions and my arm trembled, making the light dance.

What had my parents been hiding here?

The stairs creaked as I descended them with Gabe close behind me. The steps curved into a room lined with earth and smelling of must and rot. I held the lantern high and peered around.

Shelves stacked with boxes covered the walls. Gabe pulled one off and opened the lid. A few papers covered in sketches lay at the bottom. Setting the lantern down on the floor, I reached in and caught one with my fingertips. I lifted it to the light. "What are these things?"

Drawings—sketches of cylinders, squares, like a massive map of inventions I'd never dreamed possible. The lines were faded with age, the paper spotted with wax and wrinkled from water spills long ago. I sucked in a breath as I tried to read the words that accompanied them, but either the handwriting was so bad that I couldn't understand it, or the words were a different language altogether.

Gabe left the box in my hands and dug into another one. He pulled out more papers covered in scribbles, maps, and sheets and sheets of notes. Lists.

Names.

"These are mostly common Aeralian names," he said, astonishment coloring his voice. "What does this mean?"

I found something in the bottom of the box, and I held it to the light. A brooch. The little bit of twisted metal glinted coldly as I twisted it in my fingers. "Tell me again the name of that group that helped you escape, the one you said had a contact in our village?"

He came closer to see what I held. "The Thorns."

I dropped the bit of metal into the palm of his hand, and his eyebrows lifted.

It was a tiny metal branch, sharp with thorns.

THIRTEEN

WE LEFT THE barn after the sky had already begun to turn light. The sun played through the bare branches of the trees and made ribbons of gold across the snow, and the air tasted crisp. But I was oblivious to the beauty around us. My body was cold and numb with shock, my mind buzzing with questions. My parents had been members of a secret group called the Thorns? Why had we never known? And what did Adam Brewer know about it?

We reached the house together. I put a hand on Gabe's arm to stop him before we went inside.

"Please don't say anything to Ivy and Jonn yet," I said. "I need to think about this, about what it means and what I'll say to them. This is dangerous, and I don't even know if I want to involve them. And I think...I think I need to talk to Adam Brewer."

Even saying his name left a sour taste in my mouth, but I knew it had to be done. He knew something—he'd tipped me off to the room beneath the barn on purpose. He wanted me to find it. The question now was why.

Gabe nodded. His eyes searched mine, and he reached out and grazed my face with his fingers. "Are you all right? You just discovered your parents were keeping secrets from you. It must be a lot to take in."

I shut my eyes. "Right now I'm wondering what about my reality is truth, and what is a lie."

He was quiet, understanding.

127

"So much has changed," I said. "My whole world has just expanded—so many things I thought I knew, and yet I didn't."

It had been happening a lot lately, this world-expansion. First Gabe, then the Mayor, now this. I felt bewildered, newly born, dizzy. Like I no longer knew which way was up. I didn't know how to express this, but Gabe seemed to understand. He shoved his hands in his pockets and nodded.

I continued, fumbling for the right words. "It's like when I look at the world, everything has shifted. Like everything has rearranged itself while I was sleeping, and I'm just now noticing it."

"Or maybe it's just you that's changed," he said. "Maybe you're the one who's been rearranged."

Our gazes locked, and I remembered yesterday. The escape from the Watcher. Our hysterical laughter. The kiss.

Heat crept up the nape of my neck. The air between us grew heavy, and we crept toward each other in centimeters.

"Lia," he said, taking a deep breath and letting it out slowly. "I..."

The front door burst open, and Ivy hurried out. Gabe broke off abruptly, disappointment flickering in his eyes.

"Oh," Ivy said, catching sight of us. "There you are."

I was suddenly and uncomfortably aware of how close we'd been standing. I stepped back from Gabe hastily, folding my arms across my body. "Yes. What?"

"I was just worried," she said. "You have to stop sneaking away." She looked at me and then at Gabe and then back at me, and her eyes narrowed.

I blushed. "I put the horse back in the barn." The weight of my discovery about our parents pressed on me like a stone in my chest.

"Quota is due today," she said. "Have you forgotten?"

I *had* forgotten. That had never happened before. Usually I was so careful because our family's fate depended on it. Disgusted with myself, I stalked past her into the house without answering. She followed.

"Do you want me to take it this time?"

"No," I said, gathering up the sack and smoothing a hand over my hair. "I'll take it. I have to go into town anyway."

I needed to talk to Adam Brewer and I needed to talk to him soon.

~

When I reached the outskirts of the village, I realized something was different, but it took a moment for me to place exactly what it was.

The streets were almost empty.

This was unheard of for a quota day. Usually the town bustled with people coming and going with their sacks and barrels. I moved down the street slowly, past empty store fronts as my feet crunched on the snow. Where was everyone?

I found the quota master standing outside the Assembly Hall, his face pulled in a frown. I stepped straight up to him and presented my sack. He snatched it, muttering, and barely glanced at the contents as he thrust the allotted supply sack at me. I accepted it and turned to go.

"You there!"

I turned back. The quota master had not spoken. It was someone else.

My heart froze, then dropped like a stone.

A Farther stood in the street, his shoulders thrown back and his strange garments glimmering in the weak sunlight. His black eyes swept over me and my pitiful sack, and then he strode toward me.

Terror struck me like a lightning bolt. I couldn't move. Farthers? Here in the village?

They were looking for Gabe.

No, no, no...it couldn't be that. They couldn't know. It was something else—it had to be.

"Why aren't you at the meeting?" he demanded.

"The—the meeting?" I struggled to remain calm. What if my expression gave me away? What if he guessed that I had Gabe at my farm? Shock had all but immobilized me, otherwise I might have run.

The Farther looked disgusted with my question. "Your whole village was ordered to assemble by your leader." He pointed at the door to the Assembly Hall. "Get inside now before you suffer the repercussions of disobedience."

The Farther had a gun in his hands. The quota master turned his head and acted as though he heard nothing. What else could I do?

I crossed the road to the Assembly Hall.

The door creaked as I tugged it open, and my eyes widened. Villagers packed the place, crowding on the benches and lining the walls. I'd never seen so many here at one time. I stepped inside, looking around for a place, and a woman scooted over to give me room to sit. Gratefully I sank down beside her. A few heads turned to look at me, but most were fixated on the front of the room.

My nerves sang with the tension in the room—it was as if every breath was held while we waited for air.

The Mayor stood before everyone, flanked on either side by Farthers dressed in their strange gray clothing and carrying gleaming rifles. They gazed at us, arms crossed, and the crowd cowered beneath their stares like mice. Whispers buzzed throughout the room.

"Quiet," the Mayor barked, his voice tense and high with fear. "We have nothing to worry about. These men are here to find one of their own, one who escaped and headed into the Frost several weeks ago." He lifted his hand, and something gleamed in the light. "This was found here this morning. It's a tracking device. It was on the prisoner they're searching for."

Dread spread through me like a poison, paralyzing my limbs and stealing my breath.

It was the bit of metal I'd dug from Gabe's back and later thrown in the creek.

I wanted to jump up and run back to the farm immediately, but of course I couldn't do anything to draw attention to myself. I focused on taking deep breaths and keeping my expression neutral as the Mayor continued speaking.

"If we cooperate," he said, smiling thinly, "then we'll find that we have nothing to fear."

I couldn't believe it. We'd never had any dealings with the Farthers, and now they were roaming our town? Why were the Elders allowing this? Why weren't they refusing to go along with this invasion of our privacy, our property? I looked at the row of men at the front, and I saw faint, purplish bruises on a few faces.

Maybe they *had* refused.

"Nothing has changed," the Mayor assured us. "Your quotas are still due as usual. And we have a nice social tomorrow evening for the young people that will be held

131

at my house now due to accommodation of the Farthers here."

I caught a glimpse of Ann near the front of the room. Her face was pale as she stared at her father without blinking. Cole sat beside her, his eyebrows drawn together and his back ramrod straight. His mouth was pressed in a firm line.

The door to the Assembly Hall opened again, and another villager stepped inside. *Adam Brewer.* I saw the way his eyes narrowed at the sight of the Farthers, the way he smoothed his expression over and took a seat like he didn't have a care in the world. His hands, I noticed, were knotted fists by his side.

I had to speak to him.

"Everyone just needs to stay calm," the Mayor said. "Return to your houses and farms and devote yourselves to your responsibilities. Until this has all blown over, I am instituting a no-travel rule. Stay at home unless you have specific business in the village. The exception, of course, will be the social. Like I said, everything is all right, and it's business as usual. We just have a few temporary adjustments, that's all."

"How long will they stay?" someone yelled.

The Farthers continued to stand motionless and expressionless as statues. They looked like predators ready to spring at the slightest provocation. Chills descended my spine as I looked at them.

"Our visitors will search the village and the farms, and when they are satisfied that their fugitive is not here, they will leave," the Mayor promised. "Everything will be fine. We are cooperating. There will be no violence. Don't worry."

It sounded like he was assuring himself as much as he was assuring us. My blood boiled at the injustice of it all. How dare they come here and try to bully us?

A farmer on the front row jumped up, his face creased with anger. "This is ridiculous," he said loudly, pointing his finger at the Mayor. "How dare you allow these Farthers to stay here in our village! We are a free people, and they are oppressive monsters. We have no dealings with them. How dare you—"

He stepped forward, his hands forming fists. Swiftly, the Farthers drew their weapons. The farmer froze.

"Please just sit down," the Mayor said. "We'll get this all sorted out."

The farmer slunk back to his seat, but the Farthers didn't lower their guns.

No one dared to ask any more questions. The mood in the room turned icy, and the murmurs swirled around me like furtive breaths of wind. I was alone in this crowd as terror sliced at me like Watcher claws.

What was I going to do?

We were dismissed, and people began to move toward the exits. Adam Brewer vanished out the door before I could even stand. I jumped up and hurried after him, bumping into several villagers and wriggling around a clump of whispering, wide-eyed women. But when I reached the street, he'd vanished.

Farthers were already heading for the paths, their strides swift and precise.

They were starting the search.

I couldn't take the time to look for Adam Brewer. I had to get back to the farm at once. But there was a curfew now—we weren't supposed to travel beyond our homes. I couldn't be out to speak with him later, not until the Farthers left.

And I didn't know how long that would be.

"Lia!"

Ann pushed her way through the crowd to reach me. I turned to her, uncertain about what she wanted.

After all that had happened, I realized I barely knew her. I barely knew anyone. But to my surprise, she threw her arms around me and burst into tears.

"Ann," I said, turning my head to look for Farthers. "What is it? What's wrong?"

"Not here," she whispered. "Come on."

We stepped into a side alley, and she pulled away from me and put her hands over her face.

"Everything is going wrong," she sobbed. "The Farthers...they beat up the Elders. They threatened my father. They're being so cruel. They're threatening everyone. I'm really scared."

I dropped the sack of supplies in the snow and put my arms around her again, soothing her. But in the back of my mind, I was calculating how long it would take the Farthers to get to my farm. I had to get back to warn Gabe. He could hide in the place below the barn if he had time.

"I'm scared too," I said. And it was true. I was terrified. I only wished I could tell her why.

Shadows blocked the light at the end of the alley. The Mayor stood gazing at us, flanked by Farthers. Ann gulped and looked at me, frantic. "Are you still coming tomorrow night?"

"I...I don't know."

How in the world could I go to a social when all of this was happening? I had to worry about Gabe and my parents' secrets and Adam Brewer.

"Ann," the Mayor said firmly.

Her expression turned fierce. "You *must* come, Lia Weaver. Promise me."

"I can't promise anything." I took a step back, my gaze shooting from her to the Mayor and the Farthers with him.

Ann grabbed my arm. "It's really important, Lia. I mean it."

"I really must be going." I gently pried her hand off my arm, and then I picked up my sack of supplies and fled for the path to the farm.

~

The Farthers' footprints showed that they were ahead of me. I fled down the path, heart pounding, hoping I wasn't too late. Would they go straight to our farm? Would they stop along the way first? My skirts bunched around my legs, hindering me, and I grabbed them and lifted them high so I could run. Cold air rushed over my calves.

It was almost a mile to the farm, and I ran the entire way. I reached the yard, sweat streaking down my neck and back and my lungs burning. The Farthers were at the house. Ivy was on the porch. She saw me, but her eyes slid away as if she didn't. The Farthers didn't turn.

I crept to the barn and went inside. Where was Gabe now? Trapped in the house? What would they do when they found him? Would they hurt us? I was dizzy with terror.

Hands closed around me, dragging me back. I clamped my mouth shut to hold in a scream as Gabe turned me around to face him. His face was drawn and pale.

"Farthers," I gasped. "From the village, they've come looking for you—"

He gripped my arms, silencing me. "I saw them. Fortunately, I was here looking after the horses when they came. Otherwise we might all be under arrest right now."

135

We stared at each other a moment. "What are they going to do if they find you?" I whispered.

"Kill me." His throat jumped as he swallowed hard. "And who knows what will happen to you and your siblings. They're completely ruthless. We need to hide *now*."

"The room—" I ran to the floor and pressed the hidden button. The stones slid back, revealing the wooden staircase. Gabe descended it and then looked up at me. A sliver of light shone through the cracks in the barn wall, illuminating half of his face and one of his bright blue eyes. He looked terrified. "Lia?"

"Stay quiet," I said. "I'll come get you when everything is all right again."

He looked like he wanted to argue, but there wasn't time and we both knew it. I needed to be up here to handle things, no matter how dangerous these men might be.

Footsteps thudded outside, and I heard muffled commands and Ivy's voice pleading.

Gabe's face contorted, and he reached up with one hand and grabbed mine, squeezing it tight. I understood. I squeezed back, and he released me, and I touched the button again. The stones slid back into place.

He was hidden.

I straightened just as the barn door flew open and the Farthers streamed inside, followed by a white-faced Ivy. She almost crumpled over when she spotted me.

"Lia," she gasped out, her voice trembling. "Here you are. These men—"

"Are just here temporarily," I said brightly, holding her eyes with mine. Unless Gabe had told her about the room—which I'd asked him not to—then she didn't know of its existence. That was good, because it meant she couldn't accidentally give it away. "Carry on with

136

your business, gentlemen. You'll get no objections from us."

Ivy's eyes widened in confusion at my words, but I moved my hand in a sharp gesture of silence, and she clamped her mouth shut.

The Farthers moved around the room, prodding at the hay and peering into barrels of grain. One of them stepped up to me and looked me over like I was yesterday's garbage

"Are you in charge of this household?"

"Yes," I said, crossing my arms and tipping my head up to look him in the face. My whole body felt squeezed tight with terror, but I forced myself to smile as if everything were fine. "I am. I just returned from the village."

"Then you must know our purpose here. You are to cooperate with us fully."

"Yes," I agreed. "And we will. I apologize if my sister has given you any trouble—she is young and impulsive."

His eyes cut to Ivy and then back to me. He smirked. "In our land, subordinates are kept under control."

I couldn't help myself. "Yes, as clearly evidenced by your search for a runaway."

He slapped me hard, and the sound rang out through the room.

"Do not speak back to your betters, farm girl," he hissed.

I straightened slowly with one hand pressed to my throbbing cheek. This time, I didn't meet his eyes, but not because I was subdued. No—I didn't want him to see the murderous expression in mine.

One of the soldiers crossed the barn, and his boots thumped against the circle. He paused, looking down at it speculatively, and my blood turned to ice.

No.

137

He bent down, running his fingers across the etchings there. Despair flooded my mind. How had we gone our whole lives without finding that door if this man was suspicious after one minute?

Ivy shrieked, startling me and drawing the Farther's attention away from the floor. She ran across the barn toward one of the other soldiers who was poking around in the coop.

"Don't," she cried out, grabbing his arm. "You'll upset them, and then they won't lay."

"Ivy," I said loudly. My heart was pounding. I kept one eye on the Farther who was only feet above Gabe's hiding spot. He was now focused on Ivy and the other soldier.

The soldier shook her off. "Let go of me, bitch."

I grabbed my skirts and hurried forward. "Don't touch my little sister."

He lifted his hand to hit her, and I yanked her back into my arms and closed my eyes. A roaring sound filled my ears. I braced myself—

"Gentlemen," the Farther leader cut in, and his voice slid through the air like a knife. "Enough. We are finished here; we will search outside."

The Farther gave Ivy and me one last challenging look before following the rest of the men into the yard. The door in the floor was forgotten.

Ivy made a sobbing sound, and I crushed her to me in a hug. "Are you all right?"

"I'm fine—you?" She touched the red spot on my face where the Farther leader had slapped me. "You were so brave."

I exhaled shakily. She had no idea how close we'd just come to being killed.

"Where's Gabe?" she whispered, looking around.

138

I wanted to laugh. She was a hero and she didn't even know it. But I couldn't explain yet.

Taking her hand, I pulled her after me into the yard. The Farthers were skirting the edge of the forest, all except for the one who'd slapped me. He stood at the entrance of the barn, his eyes tracing the line of tracks to the house. He turned back to Ivy and me.

"There is you, and there is the younger girl, and there is your crippled brother, yes?"

I hesitated. "Yes, because my parents—"

"Then whose tracks are these?" He pointed to Gabe's footprints in the snow, which were clearly larger than a girl's. Gabe had been wearing an old pair of my father's shoes, and they left a smooth print in the snow instead of a pattern like the Farther's.

It was clear the prints weren't his or his men's.

The blood in my veins turned to ice as he waited for the answer to my question. Beside me, Ivy stiffened, and we squeezed our hands together. I didn't know what to say—all the words in me were frozen, cluttering my throat, refusing to come out.

One mistake and we might be dead.

"Who are you calling a cripple?" someone shouted.

Ivy and I looked up, startled. The Farther turned with languid, predatory grace.

Jonn stood in the doorway of the house, squinting in the sunlight. I held my breath, and my sister's hand crept into mine and squeezed tight as our brother gazed boldly at the Farther, his chin in the air. His crutches were nowhere in sight.

The Farther surveyed my brother for a moment that felt like an eternity before spitting in the snow to show his dismissal of us all. "Ah," he grunted. He'd been hoping to catch us; I could see it on his otherwise impassive face.

139

I didn't say anything. My lips felt dry. My mouth was still empty of words. The Farther glared, spat again, and stalked across the yard to join the others by the forest. Together, they plunged into the woods and were gone.

Air seemed to fill the yard again, as if the forest itself had exhaled in relief.

Ivy and I ran to the house. Jonn stood propped against the rail of the porch, sweat beading on his forehead and upper lip. He pointed to the crutches that lay in the doorway, discarded before he'd come outside. "I could only take two steps on my own," he bit out, his face twisted with pain that was only visible up close. "But I think it was enough."

Tears slipped down my cheeks. "It was enough," I whispered, helping him hop back inside. Ivy grabbed the crutches, and we shut the door behind us.

"What about Gabe?" Ivy said, pacing to the window. "Where is he?"

"He's hidden, and he needs to stay that way until those Farthers are gone." I hesitated, looking at their brave faces. It was time they knew. All our lives were at stake now, so telling them made little difference.

"And there's something I have to tell you both, something about Ma and Da."

FOURTEEN

WHEN THE SUN had begun to creep toward the horizon and the Farthers still hadn't returned, I took my siblings to the barn. Jonn limped on his crutches with our support, and Ivy helped him. They both gasped as I pressed the button and the stones slid back to reveal the stairs.

"Gabe?" I called softly into the hole.

His face appeared out of the darkness, looking up at me, and I scrambled down the steps. He hugged me tight when I reached the bottom, and I could feel his heart beating against mine.

"We brought you food," I said, drawing back and handing him the sack.

Behind me, Jonn had settled on the top step. Ivy descended them slowly, holding the lantern above her head and looking around in amazement "This is incredible," she breathed. "So they were hiding this from us the whole time?"

"It's hard to believe, I know." But as I said the words I remembered things, glances they'd shared at the dinner table, absences that hadn't been explained, whispered conversations and visits to the barn in the early morning hour while we were supposed to be sleeping. My chest tightened—I wished they had told us, although I understood why they hadn't.

I missed them so deeply now. I wished they could be here to tell me what I should do about the Farthers, about Gabe, about this so-called gate.

Gabe disappeared into the darkness and came back with a box. "It's pretty dark down here even in the day," he said, "but some light comes through the cracks. I took a look at a lot of these papers. Look at this."

It was a book of maps. I flipped through it slowly— most of them were just places around the Frost, various farms or hollows. Nothing special. A few were completely foreign to me—"This one's for Aeralis," Gabe explained, tapping it with his finger—but most were local.

"But look at this," he said, holding one up to the light.

The map was made of vellum so thin that it looked like cloudy glass. Drawings were scrawled atop the surface, but in an odd, piecemeal way—sections were missing, symbols incomplete, words half-finished. I held it to the light in confusion, my forehead wrinkling.

"It isn't finished?" Ivy asked, peering over my shoulder.

"Hmm," I said, tracing some of the words with the tip of my finger. "I think this map is supposed to go over another piece of paper. See how transparent it is?" I laid it over one of the other maps to demonstrate. "Find the right map and all the pieces will match up."

"This is the only map of the whole Frost I could find," Gabe said of the vellum. "There isn't another like it."

I looked back at the book and then rifled through the box, but I couldn't find anything that matched the map in my hand.

"It seems like an extra precaution, perhaps," Ivy murmured aloud. She was a sharp one, my sister.

"Do you think it's the map that will tell us where to find that place you're looking for—Echlos and the gate?" I met Gabe's eyes over Ivy's head.

"I think so. We need that map, Lia. I'm not going to find the gate without it."

Finding it meant his safety, but it also meant his departure. My heart ached just thinking about it, but I didn't have the time to waste on that kind of reflection right now. We just needed to get Gabe to the next step of his journey. It was what he needed, and now we knew it was what my parents would have done, too.

I examined the paper again. In one corner someone had hastily drawn a flower. It looked familiar to me, but I couldn't remember why.

"Do any of the other maps have this flower?" I asked.

We looked through the box, examining each with care. None of them did.

And then I remembered.

"The Mayor had a map," I said slowly. "I saw it on his desk when I went to speak with him. It had this same flower, I'm sure of it. I remember thinking it was odd. At the time, I had no idea what it could be."

And it had said *Echlos*.

"Do you think the Mayor's map is the other half?" Gabe asked. "The one that matches this one?"

Our eyes met.

We both knew that it was.

"We need to see that map."

Ivy had come forward to peer at the book, and now she turned and looked at me, her forehead wrinkling. "How in the world are you going to get a glimpse of a map that the Mayor has?"

But I smiled, because a plan was already forming in my head.

143

~

I stood before the mirror, gazing at my reflection, and I didn't recognize the girl staring back. Her eyes were solemn, her face was composed but white with nervousness. She was slender from not quite enough food and too much hard work, but she stood tall because she had a mission to accomplish. And I hoped this girl was someone who would make her parents proud, if they could see her now.

Ann's dress fit perfectly. The fabric fell to the floor in lacy waves, skimming the tops of my feet, and the delicate sleeves covered my wrists and rippled when I moved. I didn't have any fancy silk gloves or expensive jewelry to wear with it, but Ivy had helped me put up my hair in an elaborate braid, with little tendrils falling around my face. I'd even brushed some rice powder over my cheeks to improve my complexion.

"You're beautiful," my sister said proudly. "Every bit as pretty as the Mayor's daughter."

I laughed at that, because Ann was much more beautiful than I—not that I minded. Beauty was its own burden, and I didn't want it. I smoothed my hands down my skirt and touched my pale cheeks. "I look terrified."

Jonn hobbled to the doorway with his crutches and studied me. "All you have to do is speak with Adam Brewer and get a glimpse of that map. You'll do fine." He hesitated. "I wish I could go instead."

"You're right," I said quickly, hoping to head off his guilt before it could torment him. "It's going to be fine." I slid a few snow blossoms into the braids and stepped back, studying the effect. It was almost time to go.

144

Gabe was waiting by the fire. He stood up when I entered the room, his mouth dropping open. "You look incredible," he said.

"Nice as a Farther girl?" I asked, taking refuge from my nervousness in coy flirtation.

"Better," he said, stepping closer.

"Wish me luck?" I asked, softly.

He stopped in front of me. "Luck," he said, cupping my chin with his hand.

Heat crept up my neck again, and his eyes darkened. For a moment the rest of the room fell away, and it was just him and me. But every breath I took was painful, because every second that passed was one less second that I'd have with him. I turned my face, my eyes stinging, and his hand dropped to his side again.

The clock chimed, pronouncing me late. I stepped away from Gabe and gathered up my cloak and mittens. "I'll be back soon."

They all watched me as I went to the door and opened it. A gust of chilly air burst across my skin and fanned my hot cheeks. It was late afternoon—the social would conclude before the sun went down completely, so we wouldn't be vulnerable returning home. I took a deep breath, stepped onto the porch, and shut the door. On the porch alone, I lifted my chin and straightened my shoulders before stepping onto the path to the village.

It was do or die now.

FIFTEEN

COLORED LANTERNS HUNG in the trees around the Mayor's house, and music streamed from the open doors. Villagers milled around the yard dressed in fur-trimmed cloaks over their fancy clothing. Sunlight sparkled over the snow and made the day feel fresh even though snow still covered the ground and a chill lingered in the air. In the Frost, a little snow never stopped any celebration.

But despite the festive music and decorations, the smiles were thin and the laughter forced. In unguarded moments, faces looked haggard and pale, and hands trembled as they lifted glasses to mouths.

Everyone was frightened because of the Farthers.

I climbed the long line of steps to the Mayor's house slowly as I considered again what must be done. I had to find Adam Brewer first. I had to find out what he knew.

"Lia?"

I shut my eyes and took a deep breath before turning to greet him. "Hello, Cole."

He was dressed up, his hair slicked back and the wisps of beard that had been sprouting on his chin shaved smooth. He bowed over my hand in greeting. "I can't believe you came. Ann was certain you wouldn't." He paused to glance me over. "You look amazing."

"Thank you." I pulled my hand free and scanned the crowd. "Ann said I wouldn't come?"

"She was very distraught about it," he added.

146

More problems. I sighed. I wanted to make sure Ann was all right, but I had my mission—I needed to focus. I didn't have much time. "Have you seen Adam Brewer?"

Cole gaped at me. "Adam *Brewer?*"

I just nodded. Perhaps he was inside.

Cole's forehead pinched as he studied me. "You've been acting strange lately," he said. "I've barely seen you over the last few weeks, and whenever I do you're in a hurry, or distracted, or lost in a daydream. It's like you've suddenly found a new purpose."

You have no idea, I thought. "Making sure my family survives the winter is purpose enough, I think."

Cole smirked and shook his head. "Don't be coy. I think you've got an interest in someone."

I spared him a quick glance to show how silly that was, but my cheeks flushed, giving me away as my mind flew to Gabe and a flutter warmed my stomach. Cole noticed my blush and pounced on the incriminating evidence. "I knew it. I was right."

A sly, almost cruel grin split his face, but I didn't miss the angry emotion that flashed in his eyes.

"Is it Adam Brewer?" he asked after a pause.

"What? *No.* Are you insane?"

"Why are you looking for him, then?"

He was asking too many questions. His obsession with me was going from annoying to dangerous. "Cole," I said firmly. "I am not interested in your advances."

His mouth fell open. "I—I—" he stammered. "I beg your pardon, Lia—"

"You ought to. You've been pestering me for months despite my obvious disinterest in you. There is hopeful persistence, and there is willful rudeness, and I think you've crossed from one to the other."

147

Color flooded his face, and his mouth twisted into a scowl. His eyes simmered as they met mine. He was angry. "I'm glad you made yourself clear, then."

"So am I." But unease prickled at me. Had I been too harsh?

I spotted Adam Brewer by the doorway. "Excuse me," I said, my tone crisp. Picking up my skirts, I slipped through the crowd toward the front of the house.

He was gone when I got to the porch. Frustrated, I turned to sweep the yard with my gaze again. A few Farthers paced by the gate, their expressions cold and hard. I looked away and saw Ann in a filmy blue dress with a teacup in her hand. It rattled against the saucer as she set it down. "Lia!"

I tried to smile, but worry was gnawing at my gut, and my mouth felt frozen. "Hello, Ann."

"You came," she said, obvious relief in her eyes.

"I couldn't bear to not wear the dress," I said, but the joke fell flat. My concern was beginning to leak through my facade, and my smile faded.

Ann glanced around us at the other guests and then grabbed my hand. "Come on. I need to talk to you."

She dragged me inside past the tables piled with delectable food and drink, but I had no desire to grab anything to eat later. My stomach was in knots, and I had no appetite. We passed the musicians and the couples swirling on the makeshift dance floor where the rugs had been pulled up and the furniture pushed aside. We stepped into a narrow hallway that looked like a servants' entrance.

Ann dropped my arm and shut the door. When she turned, her face was pale and her eyes wide. "I have to tell you something."

"What's going on, Ann?"

She stepped close to me, close enough so that she could whisper and still be heard over the strains of music on the other side of the door. She started to speak, then burst into tears.

"I'm sorry," she managed, sniffling. "It's just that I don't know who to tell, but I have to tell someone. I don't mean to bother you with it. I don't mean to involve you..."

"Involve me in what?" The gnawing in my gut was turning into a panic.

"It's my father," she said, wiping at her eyes. "And the Farthers. Oh, Lia. *He works for them.*"

"What?"

"I only just found out a few months ago. He does their bidding in exchange for favors, for extra goods. He's even visited one of their cities—I went along with him. It was the most frightening place I've ever been. Black, tall buildings, lots of fog, soldiers everywhere."

I remembered when she'd given me the dress I was wearing, and how she brushed off the last time she'd worn it with a strained look. "But the Farthers are our enemies. We have no dealings with them."

"I know," she whispered. "That's the thing. It's his secret. He's pretending to just cooperate with them out of a desire for peace, but he's been doing this for years, and now he's completely under their thumb. Why do you think he's allowed them to come into the village and order everyone around? And now I'm afraid that even after they find that runaway they're looking for, they aren't going to leave." She leaned closer, and her voice dropped to an almost imperceptible whisper. "Have you ever heard of an organization called the Thorns?"

Shivers ran up and down my arms. I just stared at her.

149

"They oppose the Farthers and their cruelty, and they help people escape Aeralis. My father says that some of the people in our village work with them, although he won't tell me who he suspects. The Farthers know of their existence, but they don't know who they are or they'd kill them all. Some of the villagers, Lia! I'm scared. What's going to happen to us?"

Had the Mayor known about my parents? Suddenly it was hard to breathe. I pressed a hand to my forehead.

Ann grabbed my arm. "Are you all right?"

I looked her straight in the eye. "Can I trust you?"

"Of course," she said, her eyes widening.

"There are things I haven't told you," I said. "Things I can't tell you—not yet. But I desperately need your help."

And then I explained what I needed her to do.

~

Back on the main floor, I skirted the crowd searching for Adam. It was imperative that I find him. More Farthers stood by the doors and windows, watching the festivities almost as if they were ensuring that nothing would go wrong. Whispers rose above the music around me, and I heard snatches of conversations. Some of the Farthers hadn't returned from searching the farms. They were agitated, on edge. I stepped back into the shadows, wanting nothing more than to hide myself from their cold gazes.

Footsteps—someone stopped close behind me. The hairs on the back of my neck prickled, and I stiffened, raising my chin and pretending indifference. A Farther?

"I heard you were looking for me," a voice whispered.

Adam Brewer. I was still a moment, drenched in relief, and then I turned to face him. I hadn't ever really *looked* at him this close up before. His dark hair brushed the edges of his collared shirt. Stubble shadowed his chin—he must be older than I realized, perhaps a few years older than me.

"Yes. We need to speak."

"I'm listening," he said.

The music was loud, loud enough that I knew I could speak softly and not be overheard. My lips barely moved as I addressed him. "What you said to me in the forest—how did you know?"

"About your beau?" His lip curled a little with amusement. He was playing dumb.

"About the circle of stones."

His gaze cut to mine, all humor gone now.

"Not here," I said. "Outside?"

We wove through the crowd. My skin prickled as I passed beneath the Farthers' noses, but they didn't spare me so much as a glance. Adam was silent until we stepped onto the back porch, and then he faced me. Now that I had the safety of privacy, I continued, "What you said in the forest about the yarn—that was some kind of code, wasn't it?"

He didn't confirm that my hunch was right, but he didn't deny it either. I reached into the folds of my dress and unclipped the Thorn brooch I'd hidden there earlier, disguised perfectly against the silver beading of the dress. I uncurled my fingers, revealing it to him against the pale skin of my palm.

Instantly he covered my hand with his, hiding it. "What are you doing? Do you know what it would mean if you were caught with that?"

151

His reaction was the confirmation I needed. "I want you to tell me everything you know. Everything. Our lives might depend on it."

Adam considered the question. "How can I be sure I can trust you?" he murmured.

"We're hiding the Farther," I said. It was my very last card, and my biggest gamble.

He blinked. He was obviously shocked, but he recovered quickly and smiled as if we were just having a pleasant conversation about the winter weather. In a low voice, he said, "And what do you know of my family?"

"You worked with my parents, I think. And you must know the forest well if you spend time there. You and your family are with the Thorns, too."

He didn't deny it. "And?"

"And we're going to need your help. We need to get Gabe to safety."

"Gabe?"

I didn't speak, but he understood it all just by that simple gesture, by my use of the Farther's name. I could see him putting all the pieces together in his head, and then his jaw flexed as he considered his words.

"Emotions complicate things, Lia. Are you sure you can do what needs to be done without flinching?"

"I can do anything I set my mind to," I said. "Now are you going to help me or not?"

"What did you have in mind?"

"He needs to get to a place called Echlos. Ever heard of it?"

Adam's expression told me that he had indeed heard of it. His eyes widened lightly and his jaw flexed. "We don't know where it is," he said finally. "Your parents had most of the maps, and they lost that one the

152

night..." He broke off. "Well, it's safe to say the map we need is gone now."

The mention of their deaths sent pain through my chest, but I pressed on. "I know. But I have a plan. I think I know where to find it."

~

Ann found me by the refreshments. She slipped up beside me and squeezed my arm, the arranged signal.

She'd been successful.

The Mayor was giving a speech, and the partygoers had gathered around him to listen. Together, we slipped away from the rest and toward the stairs. A few of the Farthers' eyes followed us, but they looked bored. No one else noticed.

Once we'd rounded the staircase, Ann pulled out the key to her father's study. "I can't believe I'm doing this," she whispered, her eyes round as she looked at it in her hand.

"Hurry," I said, taking it from her and lifting my skirts so I could climb the stairs. "We need to do this while everyone is still distracted."

The lock to the Mayor's study turned easily with the key. Ann lingered outside, her foot tapping nervously. I shut the door and looked around.

It was the same as it had been before—bookshelves, a tall window letting in pale light, the massive desk covered in papers. I went to the desk and pushed the missives and letters aside, looking for the map. But it was missing.

Biting my lip, I looked around. Where could he have put it? In one of the books on the shelf? In one of the desk drawers? Panic squeezed at me—what if I couldn't find it?

153

I braced myself against the desk, and my fingers brushed a tiny button. Thinking of the stones in our barn, I pressed it.

The top of the desk slid back, revealing a hollow space stuffed with papers. I rifled through them quickly, and my breath caught in my chest as I saw dozens of reports to the Farthers with the Mayor's signature on the bottom. He'd been seeking the Thorns for them. He'd been spying on his own people with the intent to betray. What had happened to staying out of other people's problems? And it looked like he'd been handsomely compensated in return—some of the papers detailed the extra supplies he'd received in payment: sugar, expensive fabrics, furniture and meats and trips into Aeralis.

I found the map at the bottom of the pile. I unfolded it and spread it across the top of the desk, my eyes searching the scrawls for the mention of Echlos. I didn't dare try to take it. I had to copy everything, and quickly. Pulling the thin paper I'd brought from my sleeve of my dress, I pressed it down over the map. I traced the locations as closely to the original as I could manage.

"Lia?" Ann called from the other side of the door. "Hurry up. I think I hear someone coming."

I worked faster. When I finished, I shoved the map back in the secret compartment and pressed the button to close it. I ran to the door.

"Find it?" Ann asked. She bit her lip and looked over her shoulder as I eased the door closed behind me. Someone was coming—I could hear the thump of their footsteps.

I nodded. "I found it. Let's go."

We smoothed our skirts and walked slowly, angling our heads down as if we were sharing a secret.

A pair of Farthers passed us in the hall, speaking in low tones. They didn't look at our faces, and a murmur of their conversation reached my ears as we passed them.

"...Make another sweep of the farms tomorrow," one was saying. "We've received a tip about that one family, the Weavers. We're going to tear their property apart looking for that little bastard as soon as it's light again. Tell the others."

Coldness sliced through me while Ann gasped softly at the mention of us. I grabbed her hand and squeezed hard, reminding her to be silent. They didn't know who we were. It took everything in me to keep walking calmly.

Someone had betrayed us.

My mind immediately went to Adam Brewer. But that couldn't be right...could it? He'd told me where to find the Thorn things. He'd helped us already.

I just didn't know what to believe.

When we'd reached the staircase, Ann crumpled against the rail.

"Lia, your family. Do you think it was my father who told them...?"

"I don't know. But that doesn't matter right now." I felt frozen in calm, but perhaps it was just shock. My hands were clammy and shaking, but my voice was steady. "I know what I have to do."

Either way, I had the map. Now I just had to get Gabe to safety. I couldn't leave him in the secret room again—they'd almost discovered it last time, and I knew with a fierce certainty that they'd be even more thorough this time. No, we had to move tonight.

"I'm so frightened," she sobbed. "Father's caught like a rat in a trap with this Farther business, and you— what will happen to you and your family?"

155

"Don't worry about me," I said. I was already calculating how much time we would have, what would have to be done. If they were coming to tear our home apart looking for Gabe, then we'd have to get him out tonight. "I have a plan."

"They're ruthless, Lia," she said. "Once, when I was in their city, I saw a group of them kill a man because he'd spat on their shoes."

A shudder ran down my spine. "I'll be careful. I promise. We'll take care of everything tonight."

She grabbed my sleeve, stopping me as I turned. "What if they catch you?"

I couldn't think about that right now. If I let myself feel the fear that lapped at the edges of my mind, I'd never move. "I'll be careful," I repeated.

Her fingers slipped down my sleeve to my hand, and she squeezed my palm in goodbye.

"Thank you for helping me, Ann," I whispered.

She nodded, and her lip quivered. "I'm sorry I can't do more."

I smiled at her—my brave, best friend. Through the windows, I could see the sky was beginning to turn golden-orange. Night was approaching. "I need to get going," I said.

"Be safe."

Her smile was breaking into pieces as she pressed my hand with hers.

I went to find Adam. I had to tell him that plans had changed—we had to take Gabe tonight.

156

SIXTEEN

LEAVING THE PARTY, I moved down the village road and toward the forest as fast I as could without attracting attention. Snow had begun to fall thick and fast, a wall of white between me and the rest of the world. The sky was slate gray and the trees just slashes of black on either side of me. I walked fast, my breath coming in gasps of icy-cold air as I struggled forward. I had to hurry.

A shadow drifted to my right—Adam—but we didn't speak, didn't acknowledge each other. When we came to the fork in the path, he paused. His eyes met mine once. I didn't say anything. He didn't either.

We parted a moment later, and I turned my head to look after him. He was walking fast, his head down and the wind whipping his cloak around his shoulders. I dragged in another deep breath and went on alone.

~

I crested the hill to the farm just as the sunset glowed and the treetops caught fire. Most would not describe the Frost as beautiful, but I saw beauty in that moment. The farm spread out below me, and I paused as I took a long look at the life my parents had built here, with the crumbling, whitewashed house, the ramshackle barn, the paddock and well, and the perimeter of trees that surrounded it all like the hovering hands of a frozen enemy. The whole thing seemed so fragile, as if it were all built of eggshells and dreams atop the ice. And I reflected that I could destroy it all with what we were doing, but I knew with a fierce and terrible certainty that I was going to do it anyway, and that there were some things that mattered more than security.

The wind blew, stinging my cheeks and carrying with it the taste of ice. I slogged down the hill to the porch. My legs were weak with relief.

I'd made it.

Ivy and Jonn looked up anxiously from the yarn in their laps. I tossed off my cloak and went straight to the fire to warm myself. I didn't see Gabe anywhere. "Where is he?" I asked.

"In the barn, beneath the floor. He thought it safest. Did you...?" Ivy was afraid to even voice the words.

I nodded, grim but proud. "I got it."

Her mouth curved in the faintest smile, and she bent over her work again, but her fingers trembled and her eyes fluttered closed with relief. The thought that she'd grown up so much in the last few months chased through my head, and I was proud of her.

"What about Adam Brewer?" Jonn asked.

"I spoke to him and showed him the pin. He recognized it." I leaned down to warm my hands against the heat of the fire. "His family knows these woods. He's going to help us."

"But how can we trust them?" Ivy protested. "Shouldn't we wait until we're sure?"

Smart girl. I met her eyes squarely. She was turning into such a strong, smart young woman. But although her words were intelligent, careful, exactly what I might say...

"We may not have a choice," Jonn said softly, examining my face. "Am I right?"

158

I nodded slowly. "I overheard the Farthers speaking. They are making another sweep of the farms. They believe he is being hidden by one of the villagers. They suspect us, I heard them say it." I took a deep breath and let it out. "I don't know who gave them our name. Maybe the Mayor." I remembered my visit to see him, how he'd looked at me with such coldness. How I'd overheard him speaking my parents' names. What did he know about us? Did he know about the Thorns, the secret room beneath the barn floor?

I didn't mention my suspicions about Adam. If he was the one who had betrayed us, then all was lost. We could not do this without him.

I went to the kitchen and took down the lantern. "There's no time left to make plans and hope circumstances change for the better. We've got the map. Now we're going to have to move tonight."

Their eyes followed me as I went to the door. I lit the lantern and went out into the gathering night. The snow swirled around me, brushing my cheeks like fat white moths in the darkness. I crossed the yard to the edge of the woods and hung the lantern on the branch of the tallest, barest tree. The flame glowed in the near-darkness, just a flicker as faint as a captured star. Far away, I knew Adam would look through the telescope he had described to me and see it, and he would know that it was time.

After one last look at that faltering light playing over the snow, I went into the barn and pressed the button to open the secret room.

Gabe was waiting on the steps, his arms folded and his head leaned back against the wall. He opened his eyes and watched me descend the steps. There were so many words to say, so many questions to ask, but he didn't say any of them. He just watched me, and the pain

159

splintering in my chest was almost unbearable. I sank to the ground beside him and put my head back against the wall beside his. The air around us seemed close, warm, and sparks crackled between the places where our arms almost touched.

"It went well," I said, finally. "Ann helped me get inside the Mayor's office, and I found the map. I spoke to Adam Brewer, and they agreed to help us. Everything is going according to plan."

He turned his head a little so he was looking me straight in the eye, and the look in his eyes split me in half. "Then why are you so unhappy?"

The sting started behind my eyes. I blinked, keeping it at bay. "Have you ever felt that it's just too dangerous to love people?"

He was quiet. Something glistened in his eye.

"My parents, and now you." I realized too late my confession, and I glanced at him quickly. He reached out to touch my cheek, and I rushed on. "I keep losing people. Well, sometimes I wonder if it's worth it. Is this struggle to *feel* worth it? I just keep bleeding and bleeding, and it seems like it never stops."

"Lia, what if—" he started, but I put my hand against his mouth. If I heard his words I might not be able to continue.

"You've got to leave tonight," I said, my throat tight. *And I don't want you to,* I thought. But those words were best left unspoken, perhaps. "The Farthers are coming again to the farm tomorrow, after the danger of the Watchers has passed. I heard them saying it at the social. We don't have much time."

A single tear slipped down my face and fell like a raindrop. His thumb brushed the wet trail it left behind, and he said my name so gently I thought I was going to break.

"You're right," he said. "It's not safe for you if I stay. And there's no life for me here."

"I know," I said. "I know all of that. But knowing doesn't make it easier."

He kissed me at first like he was afraid I'd break, and then he kissed me like it was the last thing he'd ever do.

~

The world outside was black, the sky cloudy but free of snow when we left the barn. The lantern glowed against the snow and threw the trees around it into sharp relief. I saw a flicker of movement in the forest, a ripple of fur and claws that melted against the darkness so quickly that I might have only imagined it. A trickle of cold anticipation slid down my back and made me shiver.

We slipped inside the house. Ivy had a bag of food packed, and she handed it to Gabe wordlessly. Everyone suddenly had nothing to say. Ivy hugged him tight, and he and Jonn clasped hands. I hovered by the door, tense and full of roiling emotions. Taking a deep breath, I pinned the brooch belonging to my parents to my cloak. If we were caught with Gabe in the woods, they'd know who we were anyway. Wearing it made me feel closer to my parents.

We finished our goodbyes. Ivy was openly crying now, the tears dripping off her chin. Jonn's face had taken on a grayish quality. They huddled together by the fire, watching us, willing us safety in their silence. They looked so small and shrunken, and I turned away and went to the door so I didn't have to see the terror in their eyes.

161

Somehow, I was glad to be the one going. Waiting here, straining at every hour for the sound of returning footsteps seemed the cruelest task of all.

Gabe wrapped himself in one of my father's old gray cloaks, accepted the sack of food from Ivy, and took a handful of the snow blossoms from the bundle drying at the fireside. He joined me by the door, and together we went out into the yard.

By the tree, under the light, I saw Adam and one of his brothers waiting, their faces hidden beneath their cloaks. I breathed out in a sigh. Part of me had feared they would be accompanied by soldiers.

Gabe halted. "Are we sure we can trust them?"

"We have to," I said softly. "We don't really have a choice anymore."

Adam pulled back his hood as we approached, his gaze flicking over me and then Gabe. His eyes lingered on Gabe, and he raised one eyebrow slowly, his mouth tightening as if he were seeing something that surprised him. I looked from one to the other, but I couldn't see what had Adam so interested all of a sudden. Perhaps he hadn't believed me about Gabe really being a Farther.

Finally, Adam spoke. "This is my older brother, Abel. Only he and I will accompany you tonight. It's best to travel in small groups into the deep Frost, to avoid attracting too much attention from Watchers and anyone else who might be watching."

After a moment, Gabe extended one hand, and Adam stared at it a moment before gripping it. "You don't have any Farther technology on you?" he asked.

"What?" Gabe's forehead wrinkled in confusion.

"The Watchers are drawn to it. They can sense it somehow. If you're carrying anything, get rid of it."

"I—I'm not," Gabe said. "I mean I don't."

Something about Adam had flustered him. I gave him a curious glance, but he didn't acknowledge it. His jaw twitched a little.

Adam crossed his arms and turned to me. He glanced at the brooch I'd pinned to my cloak, but he didn't comment on it. "You have the map?"

I pulled out the makeshift drawing I'd made and extended it to him wordlessly along with the matching transparent piece. He put them together, his eyes lighting up and his mouth quirking in a sly smile as he silently absorbed the information. Now the section marked X had ruins lurking beneath the smooth surface of the lake. "This is incredible," he muttered. "We've been searching for months, but in all the wrong places...your parents were the only ones who knew this location. They were the ones with the maps, you see." He ran one hand over the vellum. "This is innovative."

"It's clever," I said. "Instead of one map to Echlos, you had to have both parts. The Mayor doesn't have any idea where it is, or even what it is, even though he has one half. He probably thinks he has the whole thing, too, since his version is opaque."

Adam nodded, still studying the papers.

"Will it take long to get there?" Gabe asked.

"It is not too far," Adam murmured, raising his eyes from the papers. "An hour on foot, maybe less."

"We'll take the horses," I said.

~

We rode out as soon as I'd saddled them. Gabe and I rode together on one, Adam and his brother on the other. I'd been worried about how Adam and Abel would fare on horseback, since most of the villagers did little riding, but they rode well. I remembered that his family

163

was not from the Frost originally, and a part of me wondered what his past was and why he was wrapped up in all this now.

Adam seemed to make note of the way we rode together, Gabe's arms around me. I had a feeling those dark eyes saw and made a note of everything. But he didn't comment. I was grateful.

We plunged into the woods, and prickles ran down my arms as the branches snagged our clothing and scraped at our faces like skeletal hands. I carried the lantern, and the light sparkled over the ice and snow and transformed the world before us into a wonderland of silent beauty. Again I was struck by the majesty of my home, and with that awe I experienced a fierce desire to fight back against the ugliness that had infected our village and the Farther world beyond.

Adam pulled his horse back so that he and Abel rode parallel to us. "Stay vigilant for Watchers." His voice was low, controlled. I heard no fear in it. "They can sense our body heat, but they will leave us alone if we take the right precautions."

My eyes dropped to his belt, where a cluster of snow blossoms dangled. He had other things hanging from his shoulder and chest, bundles and contraptions that I didn't recognize. Abel, who seemed the strong and silent type based on how many words he'd uttered so far, carried similar items.

"How is it that only my parents knew the way to this Gate previously?" I asked.

Adam flicked the reins over his horse's neck, matching pace with my mount. "It's the way the Thorns operate. Every person is one cog in a greater machine— much like the village here. Each operative knows only what they must know to carry out their job. Your mother kept contact with the Thorns, and my parents

164

intercepted the people they sent to the Frost. Your father was the one who took them to the gate."

Thinking about them made my eyes mist. All this time they'd carried on these secret activities, and Jonn and Ivy and I had never suspected. I wished they were here now to guide us to the mysterious gate.

"What do you know about our destination?" I asked.

Adam considered his words. "The gate is an ancient magic, powerful enough to transport a man. You've heard the stories about the ancient portals of our ancestors?"

I nodded. "My grandmother used to tell me about them when I was a child." The portals were mythic, almost fairy tales. They'd once connected places all over the world. People had stepped through them and come out in places thousands of miles away.

"There used to be many of them in this world, but they're all gone now. All but this one, at a place called Echlos. Few know it is here. It has much power, but the Farthers can't touch it because the Watchers guard it," Adam said.

"The Watchers *guard it?*"

"Where do you think they got their name?"

I'd never really considered it too hard. "I thought they watched over the Frost."

"And they do. They are part of an older time, the remnant of an ancient race," he said. "They have been here for many years, protecting this place. It's why our village and the others in the Frost have remained so protected and unscathed by empire-building for so long." His gaze shifted to Gabe, who'd become quiet. "Those from Aeralis have their own stories about the Watchers, just as we here in the village have ours. Nobody really remembers anything about their origins. There is only speculation, tall tales, theories without any

165

proof. Some say they are beasts, some say they are ghosts. Few have seen them, and even fewer have gotten a good look."

"But where did they come from?" I asked. "What was this ancient race?"

Adam lifted a branch and held it so we could ride beneath. "There was a whole world here before ours, and the Watchers are just the tip of what remains visible."

Just thinking about it took my breath away. I gazed at the world of snowy white around us, at the feathery pines and moonlit hollows. What forgotten secrets lay beneath this icy visage?

Gabe's arms tightened around me. "In my country we called the people from this place the Forgotten Ones. Most believed them a myth. They are from a time so long ago that no one has record of it."

"And the Watchers are from that time too? How are they still alive?"

"Who said the Watchers were alive?" Adam murmured.

I was silent at that, a chill descending my spine.

The horses shied abruptly, snorting, and I fumbled for the reins of my mount as panic spread across my shoulders. Adam turned his horse and lifted the lantern, and I heard his brother mutter something and point. The lantern light glittered on the snow, and I saw the dark seep of blood and a hand, the fingers curled in a half-formed fist. A dark gray uniform clothed the arm. Other bodies lay beyond it, their faces hidden in the snow.

Adam jumped down and approached the corpses, kneeling beside them to check for signs of life. "Farthers."

Dizziness swept over me. I looked at Gabe. His mouth was set in a tight line at the sight of the bodies,

166

but his face betrayed no emotion. "The ones that came to our farm—they went into the forest this afternoon," I said. "I heard at the social that they hadn't returned."

"They were carrying technology," Adam said, holding up a few devices with the tips of his fingers. Tossing the things into the snow, he remounted and kicked his horse into a gallop. I followed, leaving the bodies behind us.

We rode on for what felt like an eternity of held breaths and anxious glances over our shoulders. I tracked every shadow, straining for movement beneath the trees that might signal Watchers, but the night was empty. The horses snorted, steam rising from their withers in the light of the lantern.

Abruptly, the crunch of snow gave way to the clop of the horses' hooves against stone. I caught my breath as pillars of stone rose from the darkness around us. Shadows scattered before the lantern light like ghosts, revealing strange ice-covered shapes and structures. It was a beautiful ruin covered in snow. Ahead, a lake of ice glimmered like a sheet of glass.

Echlos.

"There," Adam said, pointing. "Do you see it?"

Through the darkness at the edge of the lake, I saw the faint gleam of metal. We rode forward, and as the light from the lantern touched the shadows, my mouth dropped open and I struggled to breathe.

"What is it?"

"It's one of their buildings," Adam said.

"The ancients?"

"The Forgotten Ones," Gabe murmured.

It rose out of the darkness, a glimmering thing shivering in the light of our lantern, slick with snow and ice. The roof was smooth and white like an egg. A tangle of fallen trees and rocks lay against one side, and a

167

gaping black maw formed a mouth in the other. We dismounted and went into the blackness together, leaving the horses tethered and surrounded by snow blossoms.

We descended steps for what felt like hours. Strange metal supports held up the ceiling above our heads, and intricate carvings covered the walls. The light from the lantern made everything glint and sparkle.

"How big is this place?" I asked, my voice echoing.

Nobody answered me, because no one knew. We kept walking.

A space as vast as a cavern reverberated with our footsteps, and the lantern slowly and faintly illuminated what lay around us. Part of the roof had fallen away, revealing the stars above. Vast metal girders coiled like tentacles from the snow that had fallen inside the structure, framing a circle that faced us like a great sleeping eye.

It was a gate, a portal, and it was like nothing I'd ever seen before.

"Quickly," Adam said, and we scrambled across the slick ice toward it. The wind whispered through the hole in the roof of the structure, scattering little shards of ice and chilling my face. Beside me, Gabe was pale and silent. His hand found mine, and he squeezed it.

We stopped before the gate.

"What do we do now?" I asked.

"We have to turn it on." Adam was running his hands over the metal, turning his head back and forth. "There's a panel, help me look..."

His brother joined him. I didn't understand what he meant, but Gabe seemed to, and he let go of my hand and jogged further down.

168

"Here," Adam said after a moment, his tone sharp with excitement. "I cannot fathom how it is still whole after all this time."

Gabe hurried to his side, his fingers moving over the piece of metal, then and the air buzzed. Light streaked up the side of the gate and the circle began to glow with faint red.

A shiver rippled through me as the power thrummed through the ground at my feet and made the hairs on my arms prickle.

"It's time. The energy will draw the Watchers, so we must be quick." Adam looked at Gabe and then at me. "Say your farewells."

Gabe and I faced each other. This was the final moment. Now that it was here, it didn't seem real. My heart beat fast and my hands hurt from the cold as I cupped his face with them. His eyes stared into mine.

"Come with me?" he asked, timid and insistent all at once.

I thought of Ivy, Jonn, Ann. All the ones I loved, all the ones I had to keep safe. "You know I can't." I said the words gently, sadly.

He nodded. He'd known I would say that, I could see it in his eyes. "Thank you," he breathed, touching his forehead to mine. "For everything you've done for me."

"I'm so glad I didn't leave you in the woods," I said back, and the rest of the words swelled in my throat, choking me. Tears swam in my eyes.

Adam touched my arm. "Time to go—"

"Stop!"

We all whirled.

A dark figure stepped from the shadows, and a gasp ripped itself from my throat as I recognized the face.

It was Cole.

SEVENTEEN

HE HELD A pistol in his hand, and the black muzzle glinted like obsidian in the light of the lantern. He was closest to me, only a few feet away, and I caught a glimpse of his wild and desperate expression before he stepped forward and yanked me against him. Wrapping one arm around my throat, he pressed the gun to my head. "Stay where you are, all of you."

The muzzle of the gun pressed an icy circle against my skin, and I gasped. I couldn't move, couldn't think. Adam halted at the sight of a gun to my head. His dark eyes sparked fire, but he raised his hands. Gabe and Abel did the same. Gabe's whole face was contorted with horror.

Cole waved the gun at them before turning it back on me. "Nobody move, or I'll shoot her."

"Cole..." I struggled to speak as panic squeezed my throat. "What are you *doing?*"

I met Gabe's eyes across the space between us. His whole body was rigid, his hands curled into fists as he struggled to stay put.

"Pretty Lia Weaver," Cole said to me, stroking my cheek with his free hand. "I'm afraid you'll have to suffer some more of my willful rudeness until I get what I want."

"And what do you want?"

He ignored my question. "I always thought you were too sensible to get caught up in all of this, but I see

I've misjudged you. I should have known you'd turn out just like your parents."

The mention of them tore at my heart. What did he know about them and their involvement with the Thorns? "My parents?"

"Don't play dumb," he growled, jamming the gun harder into my skull to emphasize his words. "I know exactly who they were—traitors to this village, conspirators with that band of terrorists, the Thorns." He reached down and ran his other hand over the brooch pinned to my cloak.

I could barely breathe. Obviously there was no use pretending ignorance if he'd seen the brooch. "How did you know?"

He laughed. "I have my ways. People barely notice me, you know, but I'm clever. I know how to watch people, how to learn their secrets after months of careful observation. I was the one who shot them in the forest after luring them out with a forged note from the Brewers," he said. "I lured the Brewers out into the woods, too, because they made such convenient scapegoats. How ironic that they were the ones I was looking for all along."

His words hit me like a punch in the gut. He'd killed my parents. He'd just admitted it. "You will pay for this."

"Correction—I will be *paid* for this. And quite handsomely."

Tears filled my eyes as I thought of my beloved Ma and Da lying dead in the snow. Their bodies had been mangled by the Watchers. No one would have seen the bullet marks after the Watchers had finished mauling their bodies.

"Who else knows what you know?" Adam demanded. "Who knows what you've done?"

171

"No one, yet," Cole said. "I gave that map to the Mayor, but I'd botched my mission—I didn't catch the true Thorn contacts. Your parents were just soft-hearted civilians. They were not the ones I was looking for." He grinned cruelly at Adam. "But here you are, the real contacts. And here *you* are," he said to me, "working with the Thorns and making the same mistake your parents did."

"I'm not working with anyone," I snapped. "I'm just trying to help my friend."

"Ah, yes, the Farther runaway." He tipped his head to the side, looking at Gabe. "Bringing him in will surely land me a handsome appointment with their higher-ups. That's what I've always wanted anyway. Not to be stuck in this forsaken place. My parents taught me better than that. They taught me that I could succeed if I was clever and paid attention. That's exactly what I've done."

I remembered how he'd followed me in the woods, how he'd asked Ann so many questions about me, how he'd pursued me. "You were pretending to want courtship so you could see if I was in contact with the Thorns," I accused.

"Of course. But you didn't cooperate. It took me far too long to figure everything out. But I knew something was up when I saw you talking with Adam Brewer tonight," he said, giving me an ugly smile. "So I followed you home. When I saw the Farther, I thought maybe the rumors about this mysterious Thorn place were true. Thought maybe you could take me to it. So I followed the tracks of your horses here. You weren't moving fast, and you were easy to catch up with."

We were silent, stunned.

Cole continued. "Now I am about to become a very rich man. The Farthers have been asking questions about this place for a long time."

172

"Rich? We don't even use money here," I protested, trying to think of anything that would dissuade him.

"You think I want to spend the rest of my days in this frozen wasteland? I'm going to Aeralis."

"The soldiers will only use you and then kill you," Gabe said, his voice low and urgent. "You're a fool if you think any different."

"Don't try to threaten me, Farther," Cole snapped. "I know exactly what I'm getting myself into. I've been planning this for some time now."

He cocked the gun.

"Cole," I whispered, "I've known you since we were babies. We were friends once. How can you do this?"

"I'm sorry." And he did sound sorry. "My courtship offers weren't only for the sake of my investigation. Maybe we can come to some kind of an arrangement, you and me."

"You disgust me." He'd killed my parents, and he thought I would consider marrying him? "I'd rather die."

"Don't make too many promises yet, Lia. You haven't even heard my terms. But first..." He straightened his arm, aiming the pistol straight between Adam's eyes. "I need to take care of these two, and then you and your precious Farther can come with me to have a chat with the soldiers in the village."

"No—"

A growl split the air, echoing through the room and cutting him off. We all froze. All the hairs on my neck stood up. I saw Abel and Adam straighten slightly and exchange glances.

Cole's arm quivered against me. "What was that?"

"You know exactly what it is," Adam said evenly, meeting Cole's eyes. "You've heard it before."

"Watchers," I whispered aloud.

173

Across the room, Gabe's eyes were wide as they stared into mine.

"If this is some kind of trick..." Cole sputtered.

Above us, through the hole in the roof, something rustled just out of sight. The branch of a tree quivered. Snow hissed down into the room around us.

"No trick," Adam said. "Do you want to die?"

Cole shoved me forward. I stumbled, and Gabe caught me in his arms and cradled me against him. Cole was backing up, shaking his head.

"All of you stay where you are. I just want the Farther. If he comes peaceably, I'll let you have a fighting chance with this thing—"

Something whispered against the snow, like the sound of something heavy being dragged. The ice crunched behind him, in the blackness of the room. A guttural growl rumbled through the air. And then, deep in the shadows, a red glow flickered.

Cole gasped and spun, waving the pistol.

Adam started forward. "Give it up and we can save you, Cole."

"Stay back." Cole swept the gun at us all, turning another circle.

Adam froze.

Another growl came from the shadows. Cole took a few steps back. A vein in his throat throbbed.

Gabe's hand found mine again. I pressed my lips together to hold back a hiss of terror. Cole's fingers fumbled with the trigger as he reached down for the bag of snow blossoms at his belt—

Something swept out of the darkness in a swift, blurred movement. I saw a flash of fur, a glint of metal, heard a sharp squeal that as almost like the sound of a knife being drawn over another knife, and Cole was gone. There was a single, wet crunch, and a spray of red splattered the ice.

The gun bounced into the snow and lay there.

"MOVE," Adam ordered to us.

There wasn't time to even think about what had just happened with Cole.

"Quick," I said, pulling out every blossom I carried and flinging it down into the snow. "Make a circle."

"Here." Adam yanked one of the contraptions from his belt and employed it with a snap of his wrist. A metal hoop strung with snow blossoms expanded around us. Beside him, Abel was pulling out a net similarly woven with the flowers. He tossed it over himself and held up the edges for us to join him.

"Hurry!"

We worked fast, standing together in terror as the shadows rippled again.

A thing emerged from the darkness, and every hair on my body stood straight up.

A Watcher.

The shadows writhed as the creature took shape. It was almost indescribable—like a snake crossed with a bear—the neck long and elegant, the body furred and square. But it didn't quite move like an animal—the movements were at once jerky and precise, unnatural. I caught my breath.

"Look," Gabe muttered.

Another creature slipped from the shadows, this one even larger and more sinuous than the previous. It swung its head from side to side as if sniffing for us. Its fur rippled in the light. I saw a glimmer of something metallic along its back, like a row of knifes against its spine.

And then from the shadows, a third and even larger Watcher emerged.

175

"Three Watchers?" Adam breathed. "Can it be possible? Has any Frost dweller ever lived to see such a thing?"

They circled us, their red eyes gleaming and their necks undulating like snakes. In their wake they left massive tracks. The ground shuddered as they moved. Every inch of my skin rippled in pure terror as they all turned in unison to regard us.

"Don't move." Adam gritted the words.

The largest Watcher stepped close. Its massive head swung down toward us, and it growled again, a strange and terrible mixture of clacking and snarling that made every single muscle in my body pull taut with tension. The red glow emanating from its eyes bathed us in lurid light, and we huddled together. There was nothing between us and gruesome death except a circle of flowers and a net as flimsy as silk.

I couldn't breathe.

The creature stopped, and made a sound that was both a hiss and a clatter. I couldn't move. Incisors sharp as knives hung before my eyes as the creature examined us. Gabe gripped my hand.

The red light played over the blossoms, and the Watcher hissed again, blowing back our hair.

I shut my eyes.

But then, with a rush of air, the Watcher drew back as swiftly as it had come. Together they turned, snarled one last time, and vanished.

The wind whispered around us. The shadows were still. We were alive and unscathed.

I sank to my knees because my legs weren't working anymore, and Gabe crouched beside me. "I've never seen anything like that in my life," he gasped. "Did you see the necks? The claws? What kind of beasts were they?"

176

"Big ones," Adam said.

"They didn't hurt us..." Gabe continued, glassy-eyed. He looked at me. "Are you all right?"

"I'm fine," I said, my voice shaky. I touched the edge of the net before Abel tugged the fabric off me and wrapped it into a bundle. "What are these devices you used?"

"Thorn materials. They won't cross the blossoms, as you know," Adam muttered as we turned our attention back to him. "The Thorns have only bits of information about them, smuggled down through the years—the creatures have specific instructions from long ago, although I don't know what or why. That knowledge has been lost to us. We only know that they watch, and guard. And they respect the snow blossoms."

"The Watcher we saw before wasn't nearly as big as those ones," I said, remembering.

He frowned. "Apparently the closer you are to the ruins and Echlos, the bigger the Watchers. The ones that roam close to the village are smaller, more agile, more easily warded off."

Gabe struggled up to his feet. He and Adam offered me a hand up at the same time, and I accepted Gabe's help. Adam turned to look at the gate.

"Hurry," he said. "The gate is primed, and those Watchers will return before long. It's time."

We turned. The eye had opened—glowing seams of red and orange bathed us in a spiderweb of light. The air throbbed with a low current of sound, like a great heartbeat.

Gabe and I faced each other. He looked at me like I was made of unbearable light and I was blinding him.

"I won't ever forget you, Lia Weaver," he said softly.

"And I won't forget you." I realized I didn't even know his last name, and I opened my mouth to ask. But

177

he kissed me fiercely before I could get the words out. I forgot them as he touched his forehead to mine, and then he stepped away from me and toward to the gate, our hands sliding apart until we were touching only air. A sob caught in my throat.

"May you have clear skies home," I whispered, choking on my tears.

He nodded gravely.

Adam stepped beside me. "It will be quick, I've heard," he murmured. "Prepare yourself—"

"Wait," I shouted. "Gabe, I—"

The gate snapped shut, covering Gabe like a flower folding up on itself, and a wind rushed over us.

He was gone.

EIGHTEEN

THE REST OF the words lay on my tongue, unspoken. I hugged myself, closing my eyes. Grief was already seeping into my veins, but I couldn't process anything I was feeling yet.

"It gets easier," Adam said. His voice was surprisingly gentle.

I opened my eyes and looked at him. He stood a few feet away, his hand on the panel that had made the gate spring to life, his hair blowing in the wind. Abel stood beside him. They looked so alike, and I was struck by the nobleness in their eyes as they drew back a few paces, giving me space to feel my sorrow.

After another moment of breathing in and out, I straightened and approached them. I might be head over heels for a boy, something I'd never foreseen happening to me, but I hadn't turned wholly stupid. It was dangerous here.

"We should go," I said, and he nodded.

We headed back for the horses.

~

We returned to the house. Ivy and Jonn hovered, curious but quiet, as I stepped inside with Adam and Abel.

"The Farthers will be very angry when they can't find him," Adam said to me. "And I suspect that they

179

won't clear out as quickly as the Mayor is promising. You might want to lay low for a while."

Coldness gripped me. "Do you think they're going to try to extend their reach to the Frost?"

"I don't know," he said. "Before now, fear of the Watchers kept them out. But they've grown bolder. I don't know what will happen."

I nodded. "Thank you for your help."

I fumbled for the brooch I'd pinned to my cloak. It had been nonsensical to wear it, perhaps, but I'd felt stronger, closer to my parents with it resting above my heart. I held it out to him. "Here. I guess this is yours." It almost hurt to relinquish it. My hand trembled.

But Adam didn't take it. "No," he said. "You'll need it." He met my eyes squarely. "We may have saved one life tonight, but there are many more who'll need assistance in the coming months, more now than ever if the Farthers are expanding their reach."

He left the question unspoken.

I hesitated, then closed my fingers back over the broach.

Adam's mouth curved slightly in a smile.

~

After they slipped out into the night again, I hugged my siblings goodnight and went to my room. I didn't really feel like talking. All the words were still bottled up inside my chest, threatening to burst loose if I let them. My mind traced the moment of Gabe's disappearance again and again, and each time I revisited the scene mentally shivers ran over my skin and a sick feeling twisted inside me. What had happened? Where had he gone? He could be anywhere now. He could be dead.

I didn't know if I'd ever see him again.

180

I lingered in the doorway, my cheek against the cool wood frame of the door and a thousand fragments of emotion swirling in me. I'd allowed myself to feel love—yes, love—for another person in a way I'd once sworn to myself that I never would. I'd become completely vulnerable, and now I'd been torn apart with hurt and catapulted onto a path I might never have taken otherwise. I'd risked my life for an outsider. For a stranger. Worse, I had a feeling I was going to do it again.

My fingers brushed over the Thorns brooch, which was still clasped in my right hand.

Was it worth it?

A dark shape lay on my pillow. A book. I picked it up, recognizing the volume at once as the one Gabe had been reading, *The Snow Parables.* I opened to the first page, and a sheaf of paper fluttered to the bed.

A letter?

I retrieved the paper with trembling fingers and held it to the light. Gabe's handwriting, straight and perfect, scrawled across the page.

My dear Lia, it began.

I put a hand over my mouth. It was an unexpected remnant of him, and it was so precious to me.

I do not know where I am going. I do not know how this night will end. But I just wanted you to know you are the strongest, bravest woman I've ever known, and that I will never fail to think of you wherever I am. You have inspired me to fight, and to keep fighting.

There was his name, Gabe, scrawled at the bottom. And then below it, as a postscript, one final thing.

In answer to a question you asked me not long ago, a question I didn't answer at the time...it is worth it. Love is a perilous dance too, you see. And if we stop dancing, we'll die.

Don't ever stop dancing.

181

Acknowledgements

Many thanks to...

My wonderful husband, who reads every draft and listens to every idea. Thank you for insisting you enjoy my stories, even though I know they contain far too much talk of emotions and far too few executions and fight scenes for your taste. Thank you for your friendship, patience, support, and for your infectious enthusiasm with this book and with all the books. I love you more than I know how to express.

Vic, Emily, Dawn, and Yosh, for offering support, friendship, and critique. You guys rock!

Julie from A Tale of Many Reviews, for working with me on behind-the-scenes stuff in preparation for launch day. You're doing a wonderful thing for authors everywhere, and I appreciate it so much.

H. Danielle Crabtree, for her wonderful proofreading services, as well as her kind words and enthusiasm for this book.

My family, for telling random people everywhere about my books, badgering them to read them, supporting my dreams, and being so proud of my scant accomplishments. I never anticipated the extent you would go to support me. You guys are wonderful. I love you all.

And to everyone who reads and loves this book—thank you! You are the reason I write.

About the Author

Kate Avery Ellison lives in Atlanta, GA with her husband and their two well-fed and spoiled (but extremely lovable) cats. She loves fantasy, dark chocolate, fairy tale retellings, and love stories with witty banter and sizzling, unspoken feelings. You can find more information about the rest of her books online at http://thesouthernscrawl.blogspot.com/.

<u>Read the first chapter of *The Curse Girl*,
available now in paperback and ebook
format!</u>

ONE

My father drove me through the woods in his truck, the wheels shuddering over the dirt road while the air hummed with all the unspoken words between us. The tears wriggled down his wrinkled cheeks only to get lost in his beard. The mark on his wrist burned at the edge of my peripheral vision, as if it were glowing.

I sat silent and immobile, a statue, a paper doll, a frozen thing of stone.

When we reached the gate I drew one shuddering breath and let it out, and my father put his hand on my shoulder. His fingers dug into my skin.

"He promised he wouldn't hurt you, Bee. He *promised.*"

I shifted. His hand fell limply on the seat between us. He didn't try to touch me again.

Dad turned off the engine and we sat wrapped in the silence. I heard him swallow hard. I slid my fingers up and down the strap of my backpack. My mouth tasted like dust. The car smelled like old leather and fresh terror.

Nobody knew if the legends were lies, myth, or truth. But they all talked about the Beast that lived in the house. Some said he ate human children, some said he turned into a vicious creature in the night, some said he looked like a demon, with flames for eyes.

A trickle of sweat slipped down my spine.

"You don't—" My father started to say, but he hesitated. Maybe he'd been hoping I would cut him off, but I didn't. I just sat, holding my backpack, feeling the crush of responsibility slip over my shoulders and twine around my neck like a noose.

Through the gate I could see the house, watching us with windows like dead eyes. Trees pressed close to the bone-white walls like huddled hags with flowing green hair, and everything was covered with a mist of grayish moss. I'd heard the stories my whole life—we all had—but I'd never been close enough to see the cracks in the windowsills, the dead vines clinging to the roof.

Magic hung in the air like the lingering traces of a memory. I could almost taste it. Voices whispered faintly in the wind, or was that just the trees? The knot in my stomach stirred in response.

My father tried again, and this time he got the whole sentence out. "You don't have to do this."

Of course I did. Of course I must. I wasn't doing this for him. I was doing it because I had no choice. With the mark on his wrist, he was a dead man. Our whole family was doomed. He knew it and I knew it, and he was playing a game of lame pretend because he wanted to sooth his own guilt. Because he wanted to be able to look back at this moment every time it crossed his mind in the future and feel that he had offered me a way out. That he'd been willing to rescue me, but I'd refused.

Instead of responding, I opened the door and climbed out. The gravel crunched under my shoes as I stepped to the ground. I shouldered my backpack and took a deep breath.

The gate squeaked beneath my hand. I crossed the lawn and climbed the steps to the house, feeling the stone shudder beneath my shoes like the house lived and breathed. The door didn't open on its own, which I had half-expected, but when I put my hand on the knob I could feel the energy humming inside it like a heartbeat.

My father waited at the car. I looked over my shoulder and saw him standing with one hand on the door, his shoulders pulled tight like a slingshot.

All I had to do was step inside. One step inside and the mark would disappear. And I could run home. I could outsmart this house. Couldn't I? I sucked in a deep breath and rolled my shoulders.

Maybe I believed that. Maybe I didn't. Why else had I brought a backpack full of clothes, toiletries?

"Bee," my father called out, and his voice cracked. I paused, waiting for more. Maybe he really was sorry. Maybe he really didn't want me to do this...

"Bee, I just wanted to tell you how thankful your stepmother and I—"

My throat tightened. He wasn't going to stop me, was he? I shook my head, and he rubbed a hand over his face and fell silent.

When he'd come home two weeks ago at three in the morning, the sleeve of his work uniform torn, his lip bleeding, and his eyes full of fear, my stepmother had cried. Really cried—wrenching sobs that made her double over and clutch at her sides. She almost looked as if she were laughing. I'd looked at him, and I could smell the magic on him. I'd known exactly where he'd been.

And there was a tiny part of me that knew then too that I'd be the one who would pay the price for his foolishness.

All I had to do now was step across the threshold. Then the mark on his wrist would vanish, and he would be free. Everything would be okay. That was all we'd promised, right?

I pushed open the door and stepped into the house. I held my breath.

Across the lawn, my father made a sound like a sob.

Was that it? Was the mark gone?

"Daddy?" I choked out, not daring to move. "Is it—?"

"It's gone, honey!"

I started to turn, but I wasn't fast enough. The door snapped shut like the jaws of a hungry animal. I grabbed the handle and twisted, throwing my shoulder against the heavy wood. I shrieked, wrenching the handle harder.

It was locked.

I clawed at the wood with my fingernails until they bled. I pounded with my fists.

The door didn't budge. It was strong as stone.

Through the slip of glass, I saw the headlights of my father's car flick on, and the engine revved.

He was leaving me.

I slid to the floor. My sneakers squeaked against the shiny marble, my fingers slipped down the polished mahogany of the door. I didn't want to look behind me into the mouth of the house, into the darkness that was going to be my home. Or my tomb. I didn't want to think of how my father would go home and my absence would be like a ripple in the house, felt for a moment and then gone from their minds. I didn't want to think about who would miss me at school. Violet. Livia. Drew.

Drew.

Grief stuck like cement behind my eyes. I wanted to cry, but I had no tears. I never had tears. My eyes burned and my throat squeezed shut, making it hard to breathe. I crouched on the floor and put my hand over my mouth and thought of Drew's hair, his eyes, his smile.

I might never see any of those things ever again.

Terror—real terror—charged through me like a storm. It pulsed through my body, pushing at my skin, wanting to get out. Like my own soul was fighting to be free of me, like my own self couldn't stand to be trapped here at this moment. It was a surge of blinding intensity, like lightning. Then I fell, panting, my hands braced on the cool floor.

"Stop it," I said aloud. "Stop this."

I didn't have to stay here. The mark was gone and we were free and I could go home—if I could just find a way out. The idea, planted in my fear-frozen mind, cracked my terror like spring warmth. Escape.

After all, I wasn't dead.

"Yet," I muttered, and the echo of my voice, soft and velvet, whispered back to me in the stillness. I closed my eyes tight, counted to five, and opened them. And I looked at the place that was going to be my prison.

The foyer stretched up like a bell tower. A shattered chandelier lay three feet away, crystal droplets spread like frozen tears across the marble. Light slanted into the hall through arching windows, illuminating the rest of the room and striping the broken furniture and torn books with golden sunlight. In the middle of the room, papers and quills lay scattered around on the floor. It was as if a great monster had gone into a rage and shredded the room, and then fallen into a peaceful slumber after exhausting himself.

Behind me lurked a gloomy hallway, lined with doors.

I was stuck in this house. My friends couldn't help me. Drew couldn't help me. My father wouldn't help me.

A sigh slipped through my lips as I stood to my feet.

I was alone.

Alone in the house of the Beast.